The Christmas SPIRIT

a paranormal holiday adventure

J.M. PHILLIPPE

Blue Zephyr Press
2661 N. Pearl, #360
Tacoma WA 98407

This book is a work of fiction. Names, characters, and incidents are products of the author's imagination or are used fictiously. Any resemblance to actual events or persons living or dead is entirely coincidental.

Cover art by **LILT**.

ISBN-10: 1-7320863-5-4
ISBN-13: 978-1-7320863-5-7

For Beth,

who helped me find joy in writing again.

CHAPTER ONE
O Christmas Tree

Charlene Dickenson spotted her ex-boyfriend on the corner just outside the coffee shop in direct competition with the coffee shop that Charlene had just stepped out of. He had an oversized, black travel mug in one hand, his phone in the other, and, while scrolling, walked with the confidence of a man who just assumed everyone would get out of his way.

Everyone was getting out of his way.

Stephen's hair was longer than the last time she saw him, and he was wearing a red t-shirt over blue shorts, which showed off tanned arms and legs. Judgements rushed through her head about how good he looked, how basic, how different, how much the same. Voices circled in her head: her therapist's, her mother's, her best friend Jonelle's, even her coworker Sarah's. Each had a different take on the rush of emotion burning through her, this sudden desire to simultaneously hide and call out, to want to slap him and want to kiss him, the love-hate mixture confusing her flight-or-fight instinct and leaving her momentarily frozen on the sidewalk.

"Just let it go," she said to herself, advice she was sure all but Sarah would actually give her. It had been almost a year since she'd seen Stephen. It had not been an easy year.

On impulse, she began to follow him, her own paper cup hot in her hand despite the cup cozy around it. She transferred the coffee to her other hand and tried to look casual as she attempted to both keep up and not get too close at the same time.

It was insane to follow him. She knew that. How long had she spent in her therapist's office crying? How many bottles of wine had she and Jonelle consumed while her friend comforted her with all the ways she was too good for Stephen? How long until she finally stopped trying to find him on social media, until the urge to show up at his house and get him to talk to her one more time abated, until she could accept that it really was over and that neither of them had to be bad guys for the relationship to not work?

The last thing she should be doing was following him and opening up old wounds.

But it was a small city after all, and she hadn't meant to see Stephen. The universe just plopped him in the middle of Charlene's morning routine, that same stupid travel mug that he'd once driven two hours back to a bed and breakfast to retrieve, clutched in his hand.

Charlene found herself glaring at the travel mug, the logo of Stephen's undergrad university blazoned in silver on the side. The damn thing was both a reminder of one of the worse fights they'd ever had, and that both of them preferred hot coffee regardless of how warm the weather. They used to joke that they were the only ones willing to stand up to the tyranny of iced coffee. They openly mocked the very idea of "cold brew." They called themselves "coffee warriors" and proclaimed that if it didn't burn your tongue, it wasn't real coffee.

Those were, of course, the early days, the good days, when it was the two of them against the world, and not against each other.

Charlene rotated her coffee cup in her hand to try to ease the burning feeling against her palm.

And then there was the infamous road trip, the thing that was going to reconnect them, help them get over the little things that had been expanding like a balloon between them, getting bigger and bigger and always on the verge of explosion.

Charlene still insisted that she never meant to leave the travel mug behind—just because it had been a gift from Stephen's college girlfriend didn't mean she wanted to get rid of it. He'd always imagined her as more jealous than she ever actually felt. But she could never find a way of saying "I'm not jealous" that could make him believe her. Charlene knew the cup meant a lot to Stephen and had been sure it was already in the car when they left the bed and breakfast. Somehow Stephen had still been furious, which he demonstrated through stony looks and blaring music for the entire two hours back to the B&B once they had realized it was nowhere to be found, and a good six hours after that. The silence ended in gritted-teeth arguing, which lead to more silence, which lead to angry sex, which lead to them getting to pretend for a little while that they weren't both still fuming and miserable.

Communication had never been their strong suit.

Charlene stumbled over a curb, sloshing her coffee over her hand, and paused to switch it to her other hand while trying to shake the hot liquid off in a way that wouldn't get any on her pants. She felt overdressed for the heat, but her job had a strict dress code, even in the middle of July, even when the humidity meant that her sides were sweating. She glanced up to make sure that Stephen was still in her eyeline and fished in her bag for a stray napkin. Then, juggling coffee cup and napkin, she managed to wipe up most of the spilled coffee before rushing forward to keep up with Stephen's long-legged pace.

It was much the same when they were together. How many times did they fight about her wanting him to slow down, and him wanting her to speed up? Even when they held hands, he was always just in front of her, as though he was pulling her along. He wasn't even that much taller than her, but he had giant strides that ate up sidewalks and side-stepped obstacles with the precision of a getaway-car driver, while Charlene always seemed to get stuck behind trashcans or strollers, and Stephen would be half a block ahead of her before he'd notice she wasn't with him anymore. He never said anything, but his shoulders would slump, and sometimes his sighs felt deafening, and Charlene felt small and flawed and angry, and the argument would start up again: "If you would just slow down!" "If you could just keep up!"

Charlene was keeping up now, Stephen a steady pace ahead of her. She couldn't imagine that he would notice her behind him—he never noticed it when they were together, and whatever he was doing on his phone was always more important to him than what was around him—but she also was afraid of getting too close.

Her own phone vibrated loudly at her from her purse, and she pulled it out and tried to hold the oversized, flat rectangle in one inadequate hand while opening her text messages.

I THINK I JUST SAW LENA DUNHAM ON THE TRAIN.

Jonelle's message made Charlene snort. She pulled off another balancing trick with her phone while typing back: YOU THINK EVERY SHORT CHUBBY WHITE WOMAN WITH SHORT HAIR IS LENA DUNHAM.

I DON'T THINK YOU'RE LENA DUNHAM.

Charlene laughed. I'M NOT SHORT. YOU ONLY THINK THAT CUZ YOUR SO TALL.

Then she typed back: *YOU'RE.

She got a series of crying laughing face emojis back. Up ahead, Stephen was forced to stop at a corner while a stream of traffic passed in front of him. Charlene typed furiously into her phone.

I SAW STEPHEN OUTSIDE A COFFEE SHOP AND I'VE BEEN FOLLOWING HIM FOR TEN MINUTES.

She got one word back: GIRL.

I'M CRAZY, RIGHT?

YOU'RE SOMETHING. HOW FAR YOU GONNA TAKE THIS?

Charlene considered. The traffic cleared and Stephen

was on the go again, so naturally, she moved too. She knew he had started a new job, and she imagined that was where he was heading, though she wasn't sure where the new job was. Apparently it allowed pretty casual dress based on his outfit. Somehow, that made her angry. Of course Stephen wouldn't have to suffer in pants and button-up shirts like Charlene and others had to. Things always were easier for him. Her anger did nothing to weaken her resolve though.

JUST A LITTLE LONGER. She hit send on her phone and wondered if that was true. The string of emojis that she got back suggested that Jonelle didn't believe her. Charlene shoved her phone back into her purse. She didn't need that kind of distraction. Stephen was crossing the street, and Charlene was going to have to follow suit, against the light, which she always hated. She spotted a clearing in the traffic and surged forward with a group of other, much more confident pedestrians, hoping that there was safety in numbers. Stephen was further ahead than she wanted him to be, and she rushed forward, cursing under her breath when he turned the corner.

It wasn't like Charlene's life was hard, she reminded herself, the way her therapist had taught her to whenever she struggled with feeling like things weren't fair. There were parts she really liked—like her friendships and most of her family and like 60 percent of her job. She just so often got stuck on that other 40 percent, or the fact that she was still single, or that she could barely afford the tiny basement studio she was living in. She felt too old to still be struggling but living in the city had a way of making everyone feel perpetually 20-something and struggling, regardless of how old they got. She wondered idly if she would ever feel like she'd made it, that her struggling days were behind her.

Charlene pushed herself past a series of obstacles: a mysterious, slightly green puddle, a toddler on a scooter too far away from his mother, an old lady walking a tiny dog and letting the leash dangle out several feet between them, and a business man whose brisk pace wasn't quite brisk enough for Charlene. Finally, she turned the corner, but Stephen was nowhere to be seen. Charlene cursed and pulled out her phone to look at the time, and cursed again. She was definitely going to be late for work.

ANSWER YOUR PHONE!

Charlene noticed then that she had two missed video calls from Jonelle. She hit the video button on her phone to return the call.

"I lost him anyway," she said as soon as Jonelle picked up.

"What are you even thinking right now?" Jonelle asked. She was clearly sitting at her kitchen table, a bowl of cereal in front of her. Jonelle did consultation work and got to work from home, and she was wearing a tank top and shorts, her dark braids held back from her face with a thick blue band.

"I'm not, obviously. It was just impulse. I saw him, and I just had to follow him."

"You are better than this," Jonelle said, pointing at Charlene with her spoon. "Say it."

"I am better than this," Charlene repeated dutifully. "But am I?" She started to walk while trying to keep her phone out in front of her far enough to keep her face in the video frame. It made for an awkward journey. She hated video chatting, but Jonelle preferred it.

"You are," Jonelle said, digging her spoon into her bowl again. "Or you should be. Listen, Alli's calling so I gotta go. Text when you get to work?"

"Yeah. I am so very, very late."

"There you go," Jonelle said, shaking her head. "This is more proof that the man-boy never brought you anything good."

"Hugs and kisses to you and Alli," Charlene said. "And thank you for trying to keep me sane."

"Trying!" Jonelle said. "Love you!"

"Love you!" Charlene said back. As she hung up the phone and went to put it in her bag, it went flying from her hand. She nearly toppled after it, hand grasping the air hopelessly, her coffee dropping along with the phone. Charlene bent down with a panic, picked up her phone and took a breath before flipping it over to see the damage.

She breathed out. Miraculously, her screen was intact. The coffee was a loss, but still, it could have been worse.

Charlene smiled and shoved her phone safely in her bag, heading back the way she came, in the direction of her office. As she got to the corner, she looked down and realized her coffee had splattered on her blue blouse, and she stopped again, fishing still more napkins out of her bag to dab at the stains.

So lost was Charlene in her task that she didn't register the voice until it shouted again:

"Hey lady! I said look out!"

Charlene looked around, confused, and saw a man in a neon vest waving his hands at her. She looked around to see what danger he could possibly be trying to warn her of before his words finally registered: "above you!"

Charlene looked up just in time to see a giant and dead Christmas tree, tinsel still clinging to some of its branches, dangling precariously over her. There was a single red ornament among the brown and dry limbs, and Charlene watched mesmerized as the bulb broke free, seeming to fall in slow motion. Charlene moved out of the way of the red shattering glass just in time, and stared down at the pieces, her heart racing.

"Oh shit!" she heard someone yell, and she looked up again.

The tree above her wasn't dangling so much as falling, its thick, heavy trunk aimed directly at her. She tried to move out of the way, but shock made her legs heavy and slow, and she just didn't move fast enough.

Her last thought on Earth was: "but it's July!"

CHAPTER TWO
Baby, It's Cold Outside

There was no waking. There was just a sense of dawning awareness, like a white screen slowly dimming to reveal a scene playing out: Charlene was in a small square room, and through the doorway of the room, people were moving. There was no sound to their movement or to the room at all. Charlene watched as they did things that should make noise—mouths moving in speech, papers being shuffled, footsteps hurrying past. It was by all appearances a busy office full of cubicles and people doing all sorts of busy work. But all of it was on mute. Charlene spotted a plate of cookies on the edge of a desk, and someone walking by dipped their head to take in the smell, which is how Charlene noticed that she couldn't smell anything either. As she was taking in the lack of information her nose was giving her, another absence was slowly coming into focus: Charlene couldn't feel anything.

She looked down to see her hand gripping the material of her pants, but couldn't feel the flimsy fabric in her fingers. She made a slapping motion against her thigh, which her ears didn't register as sound, and her thigh and hand both failed to feel the impact of. She tried running her tongue across her teeth, or even to any part of her mouth at all, and found there was no mouth to feel and no tongue to move. So, she screamed.

The people in the space in front of her went about their tasks, oblivious to the sound she wasn't making. Charlene screamed again in silent desperation and waved her hand in front of her face, seeing her hand, but feeling nothing. She stepped forward and somehow the floor stayed even and presumably solid, though walking without feeling her feet made her steps awkward. She tried screaming again, and slammed her hand against the wall. Her hand made contact—she could see it making contact—but she heard nothing, and apparently neither did anyone in the office space. Charlene closed her eyes and tried to think of every exercise her therapist ever told her to use to help control her panic. The problem was that they all seemed to be sensory based—counting breaths, naming things she could see or hear. They were all designed to help ground her in the present moment. Charlene realized that she couldn't even feel her heart beat, and the missing pounding made her wonder if she could even have an anxiety attack without one. If your heart wasn't racing and your ears not filled with its pounding, would you even know you were panicking?

She opened her eyes. Same office. Same people. With nothing else to focus on, she began to notice more things about the space in front of her.

For one thing, everyone was wearing sweaters and long pants, and the general look of the clothes implied that people were expecting to be out in the cold when they left. There were heavy jackets hanging on hooks outside the cubicles, scarves dangled across the backs of chairs. Almost as soon as she saw the scarves, Charlene noticed the decorations. Some cubicles had short strings of colored lights strung along their edges. There were red and green garlands along others, while two cubicles were very clearly decorated in blue and white with cut out silver dreidels on their walls. One undecorated cubicle seemed defiantly plain, the person sitting at that desk practically sneering at the decorations all around him. He was a tall, thin man with a long nose that was red around the nostrils, pale skin, and brown eyes and that looked watery and recently rubbed. He practically glared at a woman walking past him carrying a small tree made entirely out of shiny green tinsel, and he said something to her that made her look back at him sharply, turning her former cheer into a doubtful frown.

Charlene's non-solid hand flew to her unfeeling mouth as she recognized her own plum coated lips, too-thick mascara, and brown eye-shadow. It had been her basic makeup look after she had just graduated from college and was still figuring out what "business wear" meant. Charlene's eyes flew around the space with more cognizance, taking in details she had overlooked before: the familiarity of the layout, the vague recollection she had for the faces, the giant logo of the Internet search engine that would disappear during a merger two years later. Somehow, Charlene was back in the office space of her first post-graduation job, watching a 22-year-old version of herself self-consciously put a tinsel tree at her desk that just moments before she had been utterly delighted to have.

Kent Kinney. The name slammed into Charlene's brain with an associated feeling of frustration and disgust. He had been her supervisor for eight months, and he had been a miserable prick almost the entire time. And suddenly she could remember, with the same heat that was now on her 22-year-old self's face, the very words he had said to her as she was walking back to her desk with the tree she had so happily bought over her lunch.

"Jesus Chuck, did you really have to find the least tasteful way to celebrate this already tasteless holiday?"

She hadn't said anything back—she hadn't been able to think of anything to say. Her original plan had been to decorate the little tinsel tree with a light-up Christmas-tree lightbulb necklace she had found on her way home the day before, and then make decorations out of push pins. She had been planning a paper-clip star for the top of the tree her entire walk back to the office. She had thought it would be fun and quirky and that her coworkers would appreciate the creativity and integrated use of office supplies.

But after passing by Kent Kinney, she just put the tree on her desk, undecorated, and went back to the spreadsheet she had been working on before lunch. Her desire to be creative and goofy suddenly felt juvenile and foolish, and the joy she'd felt bubbling up in her drained out in one long exhale of frustration.

And who the hell did Kent Kinney think he was? Just a regular Scrooge, a giant wet-blanket smothering the flames of any amount of fun to be had within thirty feet of him.

Now-Charlene felt the frustration of Then-Charlene with such sharp familiarity, it was like she had transported back in time.

Now-Charlene contemplated that—but she had. She had, or seemed to have, traveled back in time to see a younger version of herself. At her first job, just before Christmas, at a moment of vulnerability.

"What the hell?" she said, not expecting to hear her own voice, and startled by the sound of it. She certainly hadn't expected anyone else to hear it, either.

"Yeah, Kent Kinney," said what sounded like three voices speaking in unison behind her. "He was a real jerk before we got to him."

Now-Charlene whirled around, her hand back to covering her mouth. She still couldn't feel either, but she always had a wont for dramatic gestures. She moved her hand away to try her voice again.

"Hello?" It wasn't original, but she didn't care. Because she heard the word. Her word, in her tone, in her customary slightly high-pitched and questioning voice. She heard her voice!

"Yes yes, very good. The rest will come back too, eventually. But just so we're clear, I am the only one here who can hear you."

Charlene took in the person in front of her, but their appearance didn't appear...stable. The general impression was that of a middle-aged, compact man with soft brown hair and hazel eyes wearing a salmon sweater over dark green pants. But at the same time, he appeared to be a much thinner teenager in a green Mohawk, ratty t-shirt and cargo shorts, and simultaneously an old man with white hair and a dark blue Hawaiian shirt covered in white sailboats paired with beige pants.

"What. The. Hell." It was all Charlene's brain was capable of coming up with.

"You said that," said the man, his voice both somehow barely out of puberty, deep and steady, and thin and raspy. It was as if he was speaking with three voices at once. "And I don't appreciate the language. Well, most of me doesn't. A slim majority, to be fair. But a definite majority."

His face seemed to smirk in one flash, and frown in consecutive flashes, the second a deeper and more lined frown than the first.

Charlene wanted to rub at her eyes, but she doubted she would feel the sensation or get any relief from the movement. The man before her didn't settle his appearance any, and she struggled to keep looking at him.

"Is there any way for you to…not...do that?" She doubted her own question as much as she doubted what she was seeing, and she struggled to not squint, look down, or turn away.

"No," the man said simply. "You'll adjust. Or you won't. It's not really my problem."

He seemed to consider for a moment.

"I am in full agreement with myself on that one, by the way. It really isn't my problem."

The teenaged-face, middle-aged face, and elderly face all wore an equal look of satisfaction on that point.

"But we were talking about Mr. Kinney/Kent/The Kentster." At least part of him seemed a little annoyed with his last statement, while the youngest version of his face grinned. "You remember him."

It wasn't a question in any voice or on any face.

"What is actually happening?" Charlene asked, and looked back over the office space, her eyes finding and staying on her younger face. She had never seen her own face in profile, not outside of pictures. She remembered reading once that no one has ever actually seen their own face. Lens distortion ensures that most every photo is not actually accurate, while mirrors only show a reversed image of the onlooker, and are limited to eye-view angles. Charlene considered this as she took in her tucked chin, reddened cheeks, and overly-moused and stiff bangs. It was probably not a bad profile. There was a smattering of freckles that her blush hadn't completely concealed, and her nose was straight and slightly upturned in a way she assumed was cute. But it also didn't look like a particularly good one either, the chin not pointy enough, the jawline a touch too soft. It was the profile of someone who felt sure long, straight hair cut into sharp layers that hung over round cheeks gave them height and contour. It was the profile of someone who took all the tests to determine that earthy colors looked best on her, but still struggled with blush application. It was the profile of someone who blamed poor self-discipline—and not genetics— for the roundness of her face and soft pudginess of her body. Now-Charlene ached for her younger self's awkwardness, the tension in her jaw, the eyes that always seemed to be fighting back the sting of tears. How many more years had she spent being so afraid to just be herself?

"How am I here? How am I seeing this?" She watched herself type dejectedly, and then look up hopefully as a pair of women walked by, neither noticing Then-Charlene nor her new desk decoration. She watched herself sigh and click at something on her screen with her mouse, pushing the button harder than needed. Then-Charlene didn't know it, but she'd get a new job in February, and better coworkers, and a better haircut. She was going to be a lot happier. But looking at herself, Charlene could remember just how miserable that first Christmas after college had been.

And how most of that was because of Kent "Killjoy" Kinney.

A triplicate set of fingers snapped in front of Now-Charlene's face, bringing her attention back to her strange companion.

"We're not here for you," he said. "Nor, really, Mr. Kinney/Kent/the Kentster." Again that smirk/frown combo crawled across his face, and Charlene blinked slowly to steady her eyes. "His course was already corrected. We're here so that you remember. It was hoped that this introduction, in this way, would help speed the process along. Denial takes up so very much time."

Most of him seemed to sigh, while the third part of him seemed bored and disinterested.

"We're here for Kent?" Charlene repeated.

"You remember him." Again, it was not a question. Charlene nodded anyway. "Now, remember him after."

The scene before them shifted, like someone hit the fast-forward button on it, and then it sped up so fast it was just a blurry white light. That light faded out to reveal more or less the same scene—the same people at more or less the same cubicles—with one major difference. Kent was standing over Then-Charlene's desk, a strand of red garland slung around his neck like a scarf, and he was grinning down at her. Even though Charlene knew she was supposed to be looking at Kent, her eyes were fixated on her younger self, leaning as far back in her chair as possible, her entire being trying to create as much space between her body and her supervisor's, all of which he was merrily oblivious of.

"You see?" Now-Charlene's companion said triumphantly, turning to her while gesturing grandly out over the office space in front of them.

"No?"

Her multi-aged companion was in agreement, each sighing as deeply as suited his ages.

"He changed."

Charlene looked at Kent again, and indeed, he did seem different than the Kent of what her memory told her was only a few days before. This Kent was wearing a Christmas sweater. This Kent had a tinsel garland on. This Kent seemed over whatever cold he'd had earlier. This Kent was very much in Then-Charlene's space, and being kinda creepy with how cheery he was acting, and telling Then-Charlene about what a crazy dream he had and how he woke up feeling ever so much better about himself, his life, and the Christmas season.

"He's less depressed?" she ventured.

"That man was the very epitome of an Ebenezer Scrooge, complete with trying to get your entire department to try to work on Christmas Eve. And then he became the very embodiment of the Christmas spirit! Look how he's dressed! Look at that smile! And didn't he let you all have Christmas Eve off? In fact, didn't he even invite you to a Christmas dinner?"

Charlene watched her younger self try to avoid being touched by the now-cheery Kent. He *had* asked her to Christmas dinner, she remembered. She'd thought it was a very inappropriate invitation for a boss to give his subordinate, especially after the comments he made about how she looked in her own Christmas sweater. Everyone in the office was wearing some version of a holiday sweater—it was an agreed-upon "fun" activity to celebrate the season. Apparently the pattern on her sweater hit her body in such a way that when the sweater bunched up as she was sitting, the reindeer noses made her look like she had visible nipples. Or at least that's what she remembered Kent telling her. She'd looked down to see what he was talking about, and he'd informed her that the movement ruined the effect. She'd pulled at the hem of her sweater and smiled nervously, hoping he'd go away.

"That's us," the three-in-one man told Now-Charlene. "We did that!"

"You made Kent super creepy?" she said, watching him push his body more into her younger self's space.

"What? No!" Her companion stared at the scene in front of them trying to see what Charlene was talking about. "No, he's being friendly. Just…friendly." Two out of three of his voices faltered, while the other seemed to be suppressing a giggle. "Full of Christmas…spirit…"

Charlene and her companion watched as Kent sat on Then-Charlene's desk, knocking her small tinsel tree off with his ass. They watched him full on ogle Charlene as she bent awkwardly off her chair to retrieve it while trying to keep her skirt from sliding up her tights. His eyes were still on her legs when she managed to get back into her chair, and she yanked at her skirt hem and put her hands in her lap.

"I heard that a year after I left, he got fired for sexual harassment," Charlene said.

"Well shit," said her companion. "This didn't go well at all."

And then the entire scene in front of them disappeared into white.

CHAPTER THREE
It's Beginning to Look a Lot Like Christmas

Charlene tried to move her head and look around, but the whiteness was everywhere. It was hard to track time without a heartbeat, without breath. She simply existed, or assumed she did, since she still had the ability to contemplate the whiteness, and everything she saw before. She assumed she should be panicking, but without sweat or shaking, without any physical manifestation of her panic, she wasn't sure it was possible. She couldn't see her hands, the tip of her nose, or any other part of herself, and she wondered briefly if she really had a body at all.

The three-in-one man's voices seemed to float around her like an echo she was trying to trace back to its source. Slowly the sound came closer and the words became more distinct, but it seemed they weren't particularly aimed at her:

"…not like we get that sort of information. I guess we'll just have to do this the old way."

His sighs seemed to bounce all around her, filling the whiteness up with his exasperation.

"And there," the voices said. Charlene peered into the whiteness expectantly. In the distance, and gradually getting bigger, seemed to be … something. Her eyes read it as a vague black shape, a dot that eventually got bigger and bigger until she could see that it was actually a word: WELCOME.

The word got bigger and bigger at that same steady space until it seemed to fill her vision entirely, and still it moved, closer and closer until it appeared to move through her. She couldn't turn her head to look behind her, but felt sure it was still going, and still growing. Now in the distance, more words were appearing, and a dread Charlene didn't even know she had grew as she saw them: YES, YOU'RE DEAD.

Like the "Welcome", the words got bigger as they got closer, until they passed her and she could find new words behind them.

BUT EVERYTHING IS GOING TO BE OKAY.

Well, that was reassuring, she thought. Though she couldn't fathom how things could be okay if she was in fact dead. She had the vague memory of a Christmas tree falling toward her, a memory filled with fear and pain, so she pushed it away to focus on the words scrolling toward her.

WELCOME TO YOUR AFTERLIFE! they said cheerily. These letters were brightly colored and faintly pulsing, and as they got closer to her, Charlene could almost feel a matching pulse in her chest. She closed her eyes as the letters passed through her, and for a moment felt them like a heartbeat. When she opened her eyes again, more words had appeared.

YOU HAVE BEEN CHOSEN…

…FOR A VERY SPECIAL AND UNIQUE…

…AFTERLIFE OPPORTUNITY…

Charlene impatiently watched the words float toward her and wondered if there was any way to speed this process up.

Tentatively, she took a step forward. Since she had no foot that she could either see or feel, the step forward was entirely in her head. But it did seem to make the words jump ever so slightly closer in response. She took another mental step forward and got the same result. She started walking toward the words, and that definitely brought them closer faster.

...DUE TO THE CIRCUMSTANCES OF YOUR DEATH...

...WHICH WILL GIVE YOU THE CHANCE TO...

...CONTINUE TO SERVE THE PEOPLE...

...LEFT BEHIND IN THE MORTAL PLANE.

Even with the increased speed, the rate of the words was maddening. There seemed to be a limit to how many words could be scrolled at her at one time, and it made it harder for Charlene to string the phrases together into a sentence that might actually make some sort of sense. She was dead. She had an afterlife. And somehow, in her afterlife, she still had work to do.

CONGRATULATIONS! Again the word was lit up in color, and pulsating slightly. Charlene sped up her imaginary walk to make the words come faster.

THIS IS AN AMAZING CHANCE...TO ENJOY THE KIND OF... AFTERLIFE THAT OTHER NEWLY-DECEASED...COULD ONLY DREAM OF!

Charlene sped up even faster, the panic her body couldn't feel filling her brain and giving speed to her imaginary legs.

AT THE END OF THIS TWENTY-PART...PRESENTATION ALL YOUR QUESTIONS...WILL BE ANSWERED.

That was all that Charlene needed to see. She urged herself forward even faster, until the words started to go by in a blur: PartOne:WhatIsAnAfterLife? She kept going, her lack of lungs and legs meaning that there was no real limit to how fast her mental "run" could go. Soon she couldn't make out any single words, and the constant streaming of them made her feel as though she was running through a tall forest with bits of whiteness bursting in around the mostly dark letters. Now and again, a particular word was lit up and pulsing for effect, and these her eyes managed to take in even as she flew past them:

Soul.

Pagan.

Christmas!

Spirit.

Joy!

Lessons!

Begin.

Finally there were no more words, just whiteness, and still Charlene surged forward. She could almost feel a rush of wind blow against her skin and through her hair, even though she could see neither. For a while, her entire existence was that feeling of running against the wind, pushing back against a force bigger than she was.

Then words came booming in all around her:

STOP RUNNING!

Charlene stopped, and everything was still. The whiteness in the space around her had a different quality now, less bright somehow, more calm. It also seemed to be fading from general whiteness into a light. Objects started to emerge from the light—a chair, a desk, a low couch—all silhouettes at first, and then slowly taking on proper shapes and colors, like the way the sunrise slowly reveals shadows as objects in the morning.

Charlene's body was also coming into focus for the first time in what felt like an eternity, her hand turned toward her, her fingers wiggling and stretching. She imagined she could feel the muscles and tendons moving. She became entranced with her own hand, as though seeing the bend and pull of her skin for the first time.

"That," the voices of the three-in-one man said, "also did not go well."

She looked over at him and saw that all three of his faces were glaring at her.

"It said my questions would be answered at the end," she responded, pulling her hands in and crossing her arms. She swore she could feel some pressure against her body and thrilled at it. "I have a lot of questions."

"Most of which the presentation was designed to answer," the three-in-one said. He shoved various papers around his desk with a mixture of indignation and boredom, his youngest face seeming lost in some other thought than the other two were having.

"Why just words? Why no sound?" Charlene ventured over toward the low couch, which was dark grey, like most of the furniture in what was slowly coming into focus as a pretty average looking office with no windows. She sat tentatively, and was rewarded with the slight sensation of pressure on her butt and back of her thighs.

"Sound can take a while," her companion said. "As you yourself experienced." He stared at her and her crossed arms. "Are you…are you feeling things too?" He seemed perturbed.

"Just a little," Charlene confessed.

"Hmmm." He stared at her, all three sets of eyes studying her face.

"What do I call you?" she asked. "Do you have a name? A title?" She looked him over and amended: "Names, titles?"

"Samuel Walzer," he replied. "You may call me Sammy/ Mr. Walzer/Sam." He frowned at himself, each face trying to look at the other two.

"How about Walzer?" Charlene offered. The three faces contemplated and two nodded, while the middle one frowned. Another awkward exchange of facial expressions—and Charlene wondered if the faces actually managed to see each other—and all three nodded in unison.

"It's been a while since I was assigned a new one," Walzer said. "I'm a bit rusty here. And you're advancing more quickly than expected."

"My senses?" Charlene guessed. Walzer nodded in triplicate. "Can we start over? From the beginning?"

"The beginning is not exactly a fixed place," Walzer said. "Which beginning would you like to start at?"

"I died," Charlene said, looking at Walzer for a confirming nod. "And then I came here. I'm a…" She hesitated.

"Go on, say it. It helps to say it out loud."

"Ghost?" She didn't mean for it to be a question, but since she couldn't quite believe it was possible, she couldn't help the upward lilt in her voice.

"Ghost, shade, specter, spirit, phantom, wraith, whichever word you prefer. Try it one more time, with confidence."

Charlene wished she could take a deep breath, and closed her eyes and imagined her chest filling and emptying to compensate. To her surprise, she felt some movement through her nostrils, as though she just slowly exhaled. She opened her eyes and looked at Walzer as squarely as she could, considering his constantly fluctuating state.

"I'm a ghost."

He smiled, all of his faces satisfied.

"Maybe our little excursion to see Mr. Kinney helped after all," he said. "The denial usually takes much longer than this."

Charlene couldn't say either way, having no other point of reference for finding out that you are both dead and a ghost. But she smiled back because it seemed like the polite thing to do.

"I still have questions," she said. "There was this whole thing about spirits and Christmas…?" Her voice trailed off.

"Yes, well, you were killed by a Christmas tree," Walzer said, as if that explained everything. "This really was covered quite thoroughly in the presentation."

"Please don't make me watch it again," Charlene said, moving her hands to her knees and feeling her own touch rest lightly against the fabric of her pants. They seemed to be the same pants she was wearing when she died, a thin, summer-friendly, work-appropriate black trouser. She had on the same blue blouse as well, and to her chagrin, it was covered in the same coffee stains.

Walzer sighed, which was a series of movements since not all of him sighed at the same time or for the same length of time.

"There are things I can answer, and things I can't answer. I don't know why we have an afterlife, for example, or where we go from here, or if we really go anywhere from here. I know that everyone here was once living, on Earth, same as you. And that everyone here died in a holiday-related accident. And that this has marked them, for whatever reason, as destined to be here, where they will spend their afterlife serving as a Holiday Spirit."

Charlene blinked a few times, happy to have the sensation of blinking back, and contemplated Walzer's words.

"I see," she said as a place holder. She'd had work meetings like this, where her boss would come in and discuss things with the assumption that everyone at the table had been following all the email threads and didn't need any of the context explained. Charlene had learned that if she just nodded along with the conversation, the details would be revealed eventually, and pointing out that she maybe didn't have all the information that the boss assumed she had only made her stand out, in a negative way.

She wondered if you could get fired from being a Holiday Spirit. Even though she didn't know what it was to be one, or if she even wanted to be one, the old fears seeped into her, and Charlene realized that the last thing she wanted was to get fired.

"A Holiday Spirit," she repeated. "And because I died by

Christmas tree, my holiday is…Christmas?"

Walzer nodded.

"It's actually one of the more prestigious gigs, if that helps any."

"I'm not really a…church goer," she said, unsure how this would be received.

"Well, I'm Jewish. And yet, here I am." He waved his hands to the side, presenting himself. "My mother was right—I really should have gone to temple more."

"Because…?"

"Those with proper religion don't end up here. And no, I don't know where they end up. Just not…here."

"Uh-huh," Charlene said, trying to wrap her brain around that one. "So all the Holiday Spirits are not religious? That seems…I dunno."

"Look, I have a theory," Walzer said, leaning forward. "It's just a theory, not anything anyone has ever told me or that I have any proof for, but here goes: it's all about belief."

"Belief," Charlene repeated, nodding along.

"Because I have been told that this place used to look very different. And then, in 1843, everything shifted. Some of the old relics are still about, but for the most part, this place is exactly as you might imagine it being."

Charlene shook her head.

"You lost me."

"Charles Dickens," Walzer said. "The bastard basically invented modern Christmas, with a little help from Prince Albert and Queen Victoria. All those damned trees. And those were a stolen idea too, of course." He stood up and came around the desk, leaning back against it with his arms mostly crossed in front of him, one of his six hands rubbing the back of one of his necks. "It all just builds, one on the other. The Roman Saturnalia gave us the gifts and carnival-like celebration; the German Tannenbaum is our modern Christmas tree; our Yule log comes from Vikings; mistletoe has druid roots, Nordic significance, and was popularized by the English; the Poinsettia tradition is from Mexico though it was used by the Aztecs for non-Christmas things well before that; and of course we have the Christians to thank for the co-opting of the Winter Solstice, which predates the holiday by…well, a lot.

"But the thing is, the really important part for you and me, is that it's all built on belief."

"Right, of course," Charlene said, not really having anything else to offer.

"Not ours, obviously, but peoples'. As they believe it, we—and this place—become it."

"The people back on Earth?" Charlene clarified. "Their beliefs made…whatever and wherever we are?"

"It's just a theory, mind you," Walzer said. "But I've talked to a few of the Marleys who've been around, and of course the other Triumvirs. No one would confirm anything, but they all thought I could be on to something. It's as good a theory as any, and much better than what Bryant came up with."

"Wait, did you say Triumvirs? As in part of a Triumvirate? Like in Roman times?"

"Ah, a student of history!" Walzer seemed more impressed than Charlene thought he should. It made her wonder if he thought she looked dumb. "A little joke from one of the first Marleys that caught on. Some of the newer ones prefer to use Trips, short for Triplicates. I am not as fond of that term though."

"Because there are three of you," Charlene said, trying to figure out the seams of each of Walzer's selves. It really looked as if someone layered three people on one spot, each of them translucent enough that the other two could also be seen. The middle-aged one seemed the most solid, with the younger version in front lighter and somehow wispier, and the older version in back more shadowy than the other two figures, like he was permanently living in the light of dusk. "And you're also a ghost," she said, trying to follow along.

"Yes, but not quite like you. I've been promoted. As you can see."

But something about the looks on the younger Walzer and older Walzer faces made Charlene feel like this triplicate version of Walzer was maybe not a preferred state to be in. A flash of pain, maybe shame? She couldn't isolate the faces well enough to name the expressions.

"You used to be a Christmas Spirit?"

"Ghost of Christmas Present. But that was a long time ago." He looked mostly wistful, his younger face again expressing something different than the others. Frustration? Charlene decided she liked the youngest Walzer best—he gave more away than the other two.

"And a Marley is…?" she asked, continuing to try to keep

up.

Walzer sighed.

"*A Christmas Carol.* Jacob Marley. Apparently you're not into literature."

Charlene tried not to feel offended, and focused on trying to make sense of what he was saying.

"There are other ghosts, called Marleys, named after Jacob Marley from *A Christmas Carol.* And the reason why they, and you, and apparently me, exist is because of…belief."

"Well, that part is just a theory," he said, gesturing dismissively. "Not actually part of the orientation. But you are more or less getting it. You'd have more of it if you had just…"

"Watched the presentation," Charlene finished for him. She was still annoyed about his literature comment, and it was starting to slip out. "You haven't told me what kind of ghost I am," she added.

"Well, that's the thing. I don't know what kind of ghost you are. Not yet, anyway. Right now, you're just a trainee."

"And what am I training to be?"

"A Christmas Ghost," he said with a series of sighs. "Training to be a Ghost of Christmas Past, Present, or Future. That's the part I don't know yet."

"How do you pick? Or do I pick? Does someone else pick?" Charlene felt she was actually doing very well under the circumstances and was getting more frustrated with Walzer's tone and assumptions of ignorance. Some part of her did wonder if maybe she should have just watched the presentation, but then she remembered the feeling of watching words zoom toward her and felt more confident in her choice to literally run to the end.

"Well, you shadow some of the other ghosts, do some training, and then sort of end up in one of the roles. I just do the admin and orientation—I'm not a trainer. You can save those questions for your instructor."

"So, because Charles Dickens wrote *A Christmas Carol* and changed how people saw Christmas, now people who die in a Christmas related accident end up becoming Christmas ghosts?" Charlene shook her head. "Let me try this again. I died. By Christmas tree. And ended up in an afterlife. Where I am going to be trained to be a Christmas ghost."

She paused for a moment.

"Is there any way I can phrase this that will actually make sense?"

"It's the denial," Walzer said, nodding at her. "You were doing pretty well with it, but it has a tendency to linger. Of course none of this makes sense. And yet, of course ALL of this makes sense. Life is a mystery, and the afterlife is more so. And we can get philosophical about it—and if you ever want, I am completely willing to sit with you and get philosophical about it—but it won't change your situation any. You are dead. You are a ghost. You are going to be trained to be a Christmas Spirit."

"What if I don't? I mean, what if I don't want to, or fail the training, or mess up, or just like…don't?"

All of Walzer's faces frowned.

"Then you become a Marley," he said quietly. "You get a

set of chains which, trust me, you will feel the weight of. And you wear them for all eternity. It's not a preferred outcome."

Charlene looked down at the floor of the office, only noticing then that it was also gray, along with all the furniture. Her mind whirled with information and thoughts, and all of that was hardly noticeable compared to an overwhelming feeling of anxiety and dread. Even while living, Charlene didn't like to fail. She had vague memories of the various productions of *A Christmas Carol* she'd been exposed to throughout her life, and none of them depicted Jacob Marley as a happy spirit.

The sensation of weight started to return to her body, a subtle pulling down that gave her an opposite force as she moved her hand up to her mouth, her thumb nail tapping against her front teeth in a habit she picked up in an attempt to stop biting her nails when she was twenty-three. Her thoughts made geometric shapes in her brain, darting from place to place and not settling on any particular revelation. She wondered if this was, in fact, denial. She wondered if maybe she was insane. She wondered if she was still on Earth and in a coma and if she'd wake up with renewed Christmas Spirit. That's how it happened in the movies, and TV shows, and every homage to *A Christmas Carol* she'd ever seen: it was all a dream, it wasn't too late to change.

"You're not dreaming," Walzer said with a gentleness he hadn't yet displayed. "We all thought that." He moved just slightly closer to her, squatting down so that his six eyes could more directly meet hers. "You are not going to wake up from this," he said. "I know you want to. It's the hope you'll cling to over and over again, and the longer this goes without you waking up, the heavier that hope will be, the more it will weigh you down, and hold you back. You need to let it go. This is a not a dream."

Charlene bit her thumb nail, and while part of her delighted in the sensation, most of her was still thinking in zig-zags and parabolas. If her thoughts could just settle, let her really think, figure this out, find a way out....

"Charlene Marie Dickenson," Walzer said, his voice quiet but firm. "This is real. You are dead. The sooner you accept that, the better off you'll be."

Charlene nodded because it was what she was supposed to do. But while her outside was acquiescing, her inside was rebelling, all her thoughts focused on a single word: no. No, she would not accept that she was just dead, and a ghost, and stuck in the weirdest afterlife she could imagine. She would find a way out, a loophole, or she'd wake up. She wouldn't, couldn't just accept this.

But she smiled at Walzer anyway.

"I'm a ghost," she said.

She was pretty sure she only convinced the middle set of eyes, the younger set knowing and sparkling with rebellion, and the older dark and sad. But Walzer stood up again, and walked back around his desk, settled into his chair and shuffled papers around until he found the stack he was looking for. He held them out toward Charlene.

She got up tenderly, noticing her weight on each foot, the hardness of the floor under her shoes. She reached for the papers and was relieved when her fingers could grasp them. She, and the papers, were solid.

"Give these to your trainer," he said. "He'll take over from here."

Charlene nodded again, staring down at the papers in her hand and frustrated that she wasn't able to read the thick script the words seemed to be written in.

"It's not exactly English," Walzer said. "You'll learn it, eventually."

"That's it then? Orientation over?"

Walzer leaned back in his chair, studying her face, his six eyes taking in more than Charlene was comfortable with.

"Getting you to accept your fate is really the only point of it," Walzer said. "If you have questions, of course, I am always here—though I have far fewer answers than you'll want."

Charlene shifted her weight, holding the papers awkwardly in front of her stomach.

"Through that door, to the right. End of the hallway, there's a sign that says 'Trainees'. You can't miss it. Your trainer's name is Guy. You won't miss him, either."

Charlene nodded, gave Walzer another brief smile, and walked to his office door, hesitating only slightly before reaching for the door knob. But her hand made contact, and the knob turned the way it was supposed to, the door pulled open, and a hallway revealed itself. She was about to walk through when a last thought occurred to her, and she turned back toward Walzer.

"Why doesn't any of this look Victorian?"

"Belief," Walzer said. "It's more powerful than you can imagine."

CHAPTER FOUR
Deck the Halls

Charlene tried not to think too much as she followed Walzer's directions down the hall. Thinking, she was starting to realize, wasn't going to take her anywhere good. Instead she focused more on the return of her senses, particularly pleased that she could just about feel and hear her footsteps on the ground. Other sounds were starting to filter in as well—the distant murmur of a group of people. It got louder as she walked, until finally she was in front of the door she'd been directed to. She reached for this door knob with more confidence than the last one, turning it easily and shoving the door forward cautiously, in case someone was standing just on the other side.

She peeked around the edge of the door, sliding her body sideways so that she could move through the doorway while opening it as little as possible. This was always how she entered the conference room at work when she was running late, always trying to slip in with as little notice as possible. She was much less successful at not being noticed here though, as the murmur of sound—many voices casually talking—abruptly stopped. Faces turned toward her. There were two other Trips, like Walzer, fluctuating through expressions and not always in agreement with themselves. The rest of the people in the room—ghosts, Charlene reminded herself—looked relatively normal, though several were dressed in fishnets and revealing outfits that it took Charlene a moment to recognize were Halloween costumes. There was a Sexy Red Riding Hood, a Sexy Vampire, and a Sexy…she stared hard. Well, sexy something. The man wearing the outfit was pulling it off, whatever he was supposed to be.

He, like all the others, was staring back at her. She gave him and the rest of the room a little wave and her best nervous smile. The room had high ceilings and stone-gray walls that arched toward each other. There were tables along the edges of the room with food on them—which raised more questions for Charlene—and a scattering of smaller tables and chairs throughout the space, each table and chair seeming to be from a different design era and with no discernible pattern to their placement and no matched sets. Despite the very unfamiliar look of the place and people, there was something very familiar about the vibe of the room, particularly as people returned to their conversations and tasks, and all at once Charlene realized that she was entering a break room.

Toward the back of the room, a man with dark brown eyes and short curly black hair slicked back into a perfect left part sighed heavily as he saw Charlene. He gestured Charlene toward him with a wave. He was wearing a dark grey vest over a light shirt tucked into a belted pair of trousers and looked like he just walked off the set of *The Great Gatsby*. His sleeves were rolled partway up his forearms, and if he had a matching suit jacket, Charlene couldn't see it.

She was somewhat intimidated by his forearms, which

were healthily muscled, and she could see under his tailored shirt that he had the shoulders to match. Charlene smoothed her hands down over the flimsy material of her suddenly inadequately underdressed trousers and wished her blouse was not stained as she made her way over to him.

"You're the new one then," the man said.

"You're Guy? Walzer said…"

"Walzer? I like it. Gets around that Trip name thing." His smile was wide and toothy and making Charlene really wish she was better dressed. "Guy Faulkner, at your service. No relation, of course." Then he winked.

"No relation to who?" Charlene asked.

Guy gave Charlene a steady, appraising look.

"You're not really a literature person, are you?"

Charlene felt the sting of the question and her arms crossed against the accusation and her rising frustration.

"I am very recently dead, and if I'm missing references or am not getting them as quickly as the folks around here want me to, I would think that you all could cut me just a little slack."

Guy looked at Charlene's hands. "Are you—feeling already?"

"Yes," Charlene said, awkwardly sliding her hands back down to her sides, suddenly embarrassed.

"Hmmm," Guy said, frowning.

"I thought that was a good thing?"

"Depends on what you consider good," Guy said. He looked as though he was about to say something, and then changed his mind. He lifted his hand to his head as though he had a hat in it, and as he brought it closer down, a hat suddenly appeared. It was a fedora, grey like his suit, with a thick black ribbon around it. It framed his features perfectly and gave him a jaunty look, and he adjusted it and winked at Charlene. "Come on then, let's ankle."

He started to walk away, and Charlene took that to mean she should follow. He led her through a weaving path around curious onlookers who had resumed their tasks and conversations. Charlene realized that all the people around her were wearing little badges that indicated the holidays they represented: Christmas seemed to be represented by a Christmas tree, Halloween by a jack-o-lantern, Easter by a rabbit. She also spotted one each of shapes that Charlene couldn't determine the holidays of: a vine-entwined flower, several styles of beer mugs, a wreath of candles, a bamboo pipe, and a buffalo head. She wanted to stop and ask questions, but Guy's pace didn't leave any time for dawdling.

The break room, as Charlene had come to think of it, had several doors at the edges of it, and Guy led them through one in the far corner that had a giant gold and silver wreath on it and which jangled like a bell when he opened the door. It led to a hallway lined with still more doors, each with a different decoration—giant bows, glittering trees, and colorful wreaths. There was a split stairwell at the end of the hallway with stairs leading both up and down, and Guy jogged up, passing under hanging mistletoe. Charlene was glad that her lungs were not the same as they were on Earth because she would definitely have gotten out of breath trying to keep up. They climbed up past at least three other landings, each presumably leading to more doors and more fellow spirits, and making Charlene wonder just how many fellow ghosts she was sharing her afterlife with. Finally, Guy stopped climbing and walked down another hall, Charlene pushing her sense of self in order to stay with the well-dressed man. Guy passed maybe half a dozen doors, each of them sporting the exact same wreath decorated in red and green ribbons, before pausing in front of one approximately halfway down the corridor. He opened it with some relish, standing aside so that Charlene could more easily look through the doorway.

Inside was a small room just large enough to hold a twin-sized bed against the left wall, and a small wooden desk opposite it. There was a set of three shelves above the desk, currently bereft of any items. There was a tall, narrow window in the wall opposite the door, mirroring its location. A thin, grey curtain blocked out whatever was on the other side. Compared to everywhere else they had been since leaving the Holiday Spirit Break Room, the space was severely lacking in decoration. The room's bed had a wooden frame, and a headboard that boasted a rather squat-looking Christmas tree carving, the little ornaments and lights carved in stark relief, and lightly colored—the only nod to the season in the room. As Charlene stepped inside to get a closer look, she realized that the tree looked vaguely familiar, like something Charlene's father would have picked out when she was a kid. There was also something about the ornaments, particularly one that looked like a five-year-old's attempt to make a snowman. Charlene realized with a start that she knew that snowman, had made that snowman. The tree appeared to be covered in her own family's personal Christmas ornaments.

"It's your tree. Well, one of them, assuming you had more than one Christmas," Guy said.

"I don't understand," Charlene said, looking around. There was a small pile of bedding on the chair next to the desk, but otherwise the room was empty. "Why do ghosts need bedrooms? Or beds? Or...sheets?" She turned to Guy, searching the man's face for any sort of answer.

Guy stared back, his eyes not unkind, but unflinching. Charlene didn't think he would give her much sympathy, but he also didn't seem the sort to be needlessly cruel either.

"What you need to understand is that you were human for a very long time. You need a bed, and a bedroom, because your human self still wants these things. You're still attached to the way things were, still need things to look...normal."

"Belief," Charlene said. "Walzer said it's why things look— the way that they look." She gestured at her room, the hallway beyond.

"You met with Walzer in an office, yes? Because you expect to see someone like Walzer—an administrator of sorts—in an office. The break room looks like a break room because that's what most folks here need it to look like. Complete with food."

"Do we need to eat?" Charlene asked.

"Need, no. Can, yes. But the food won't taste anything like what you want it to. And you'll never feel full, no matter how much you eat. You'll also never feel hungry. Or cold, or hot. Unless..."

Guy frowned, his eyes watching Charlene's hands, which

made Charlene realize she was gripping the legs of her trousers again. She liked the feel—and that she could feel. But Guy's gaze made her open her hands, and then stand still.

"Some folks get hungry. Or cold. Or hot. They get tired. Even though they shouldn't, even though there is no reason to. They…hold on."

"Hold on to what?" Charlene asked.

"Life. And the thousand natural shocks that came with it." Guy leaned lightly against the frame of the doorway. "Denial is a hell of a drug."

"Yeah," Charlene said, suddenly uncomfortable with the conversation. It was as though Guy knew about Charlene's inner rebellion, her refusal to accept things the way Walzer had presented them. To hide her feelings, Charlene walked to the window and pushed aside the curtain to look out. She couldn't see anything but darkness.

But she wanted to see something. That want built up inside her like the breaths she wasn't taking, and then seemed to spill out into the darkness like an exhale.

The size and shape of her little room reminded her of the little cells she saw once in a convent she visited while on vacation, and she pictured that said convent would be on top of a hill, and a window such as this would look out and over the countryside down below. As she pictured it, the darkness she stared into seemed to shift a little, parts of it lightening up to give the sense of a separation of ground and sky, and as she peered even more intently into it, the darkness gave way to vague shapes that could be hills and trees. Charlene wished for a moon or stars to light up the view. And then a silvery-white glow emerged from the sky, slowly turning up like the dimmer switch on a lamp, while pinpoints of light began to pop into existence around it. Startled, Charlene jumped back, dropping the curtain and obscuring the view.

"See something?" Guy asked. Charlene turned and shook her head. She didn't want to try to explain what she just saw. She had the distinct impression that Guy wouldn't approve. Guy sighed, and kept his gaze steady, as though waiting for Charlene to recant her head shake. A beat. Another. When it was clear that Charlene wasn't going to budge, Guy stood up straight again in a movement so fluid, Charlene couldn't track it.

"You can come back here any time you're not training," Guy said. "You can put the blankets on the bed. Put books on the shelves. Make it really homey, if you want to."

Guy's tone didn't make it seem as though he approved of the idea of homey.

"You also never have to come back here again, if you don't want to," he said. "You don't really have any need for a room. Not anymore."

Charlene took a step back, her hand reaching out almost protectively toward the back of the chair. Her gesture and her intent didn't seem the least bit lost on Guy.

"Either way, it's time to move on from here," he said, turning sharply on his heel and heading back down the hallway. Charlene had to scramble to keep up, sudden panic making her try to mark the location of her room as best as she could, counting doorways as they passed them so that she could remember which one was hers. Why this hallway had all the same decorations when none of the others did confused her.

"Don't worry," Guy said over his shoulder. "You'll always be able to find it. If you get good enough, you won't even have to walk as far in the future."

Charlene had no idea what to make of that comment, and didn't have time to think about it either as the two made their way through a maze of corridors, and up and then down several flights of stairs, the decorations changing wildly from place to place, but all in the Christmas theme.

"Is it really this far?" Charlene asked, getting annoyed by how complicated the route was becoming. She had long lost track of which stairs and which hallways she would need to take to get back to her room.

"No," Guy said, and stopped abruptly in front of a pale white door, a large unadorned fir tree emblazoned on the outside of it. "But you'll have to work through some of that denial if you want to get back to your 'homey'." He seemed very pleased with himself, and Charlene fought the urge to snarl in disgust. Guy grinned back, which made Charlene believe that she maybe didn't do as good a job of controlling her expression as she thought she did.

Guy shoved open the tree door and swept his hand toward the entrance in an elaborate gesture of welcome.

"The Hall of Christmas Spirits awaits on the other side," he told Charlene, bowing slightly. There was the faint sound of jingling bells coming through the doorway, and Charlene hesitated only slightly before stepping through.

CHAPTER FIVE
Fairytale of New York

"It's Central Park!" Charlene exclaimed as she stepped through the door and took in the sights. The park was covered in a thick layer of snow, and street lamps and colored lights cast merry shadows over everything. She was looking at the park from Columbus Circle, and she half turned, almost expecting to see the familiar Columbus monument behind her.

And then, instead of the door she just stepped out of, she saw the familiar tall spire of the Columbus monument behind her. She saw Guy, still standing near her and sporting an annoyingly bemused—and handsome—expression. He had a suit jacket on that he wasn't wearing before, a subtle acknowledgement of the weather, though he still looked like a man out of a different era. Everything else was New York City on a snowy winter's day sometime before Christmas. Charlene turned around slowly, confirming her 360 degree view of one of the most iconic parts of the city she called home.

"I don't understand," she said. "Are all these people ghosts?"

Cars were moving past in a thick stream, pedestrians hurrying along the sidewalks, voices chattering, the city clanging with all the usual urban sounds.

"Central Park, huh?" Guy asked, turning around to take

in the view. "I prefer Harlem, myself. But then, this wasn't the New York of my day. It got shinier." He adjusted his hat to get a better look.

He seemed impressed.

Charlene stepped toward the edge of the sidewalk, some internal instinct wanting to reach out a hand and hail a passing cab. Then she would give her address—never mind how much it would cost—and head home to Brooklyn. Then she could put this whole nasty business about dying and being a ghost behind her.

Something caught the corner of her eye and a sound very unlike the chime of bells caught her ears. Charlene turned toward it, still wrapped up in the overwhelming desire to go home, and was entirely unprepared for what she saw.

A vaguely gray and translucent figure was clamoring toward Charlene. Roughly female, the shape of her was nearly completely obscured by a long chain wound about her body and dragging behind her like a veil. Among the thick chain links were various items all wrought in steel: purses and books and shoes and hats. The chain looked impossible to carry, and the ends of it dragged heavily against the city concrete, tracking snow drifts with it.

Charlene looked around to see who else saw what she was seeing, but all the other people continued about their way as though nothing unusual was happening. Typical New York, Charlene thought, turning her attention back to the woman. She was closer now and Charlene could see that she was relatively young—younger than her at least, tall and lean, and through the vague sheen of silver that seemed to coat the woman, Charlene could make out long curly hair, strong features, and a full mouth that, despite the chains, was turned up in a smile. She was dressed in a dress, heels, and hat, like she had just left set of *Casablanca*.

"New York City!" the woman said as she got within ear shot. She had to speak up a little to be heard over the sound of her dragging chains, and she waited until she was close enough to stand still before continuing. "Well isn't this swell? I never really left Chicago. And this looks a bit different than what I would have seen anyway." She looked around appreciatively.

"What you would have seen?" Charlene looked back over at Guy, who continued to look amused and unhelpful. She looked back at the strange woman, her eyes lingering over the chain entwined around her, clashing with her wide-brimmed hat and heels.

"What's the matter, haven't you seen a Marley before?"

"I don't think she has," Guy offered. "We didn't pass any others on our way here."

"Then I guess I get to be THE Marley for her," the woman said. "Though you can call me Shelley." She smiled and made a slight bowing gesture toward Charlene, causing several parts of her chain to clink together and making Charlene wince.

"As in Jacob Marley?" Charlene asked, finally remembering what Walzer had said about Marleys.

"Indeed indeed," Shelley said. "So let's do this official-like. What's your name, honey?"

"Charlene Dickenson," she said.

"Sweet," Shelley said. She cleared her throat, and when she spoke again, her voice was a good two octaves lower, rumbling and deep for a woman. "Charlene Dickenson, 'I am here tonight to warn you that you have yet a chance and hope of escaping my fate.'" Then she grinned, ruining the menace of her words. "To do it right, I'd be someone you already knew, but at least I got the phrase right."

"Well delivered," Guy said, nodding approval. "You have anyone left to say it to?"

"Got a great-niece that's still kicking around. A few fellas from secondary school. All my close kin is already gone though." She didn't seem to Charlene to be too sad by the thought. "My chances for Marley-ing it up are getting fewer and fewer."

"What do you mean?" Charlene asked.

"You're not really into literature, are you?" she asked back. Guy snorted.

"She gets offended if you ask her that," he said. Charlene worked to control her face again, managing to only slightly glare at them both.

"I know who Jacob Marley is, and I've read *A Christmas Carol*, but it was a book, one that was made into tons of movies, plays, and very special TV episodes, but just a book. It wasn't a 'guide to the afterlife'. It didn't answer any of my questions. And now, neither are you." Charlene turned and walked a few feet away from Guy and Shelley. Her desire to jump into a cab was growing. Or she could take the train. She didn't have any money, but just this once she'd be willing to jump the turnstile, or wait and ask someone leaving to swipe her in. Hell, despite the cold and the snow and the dark, she could just walk home.

Home. The word made Charlene ache. She was so close.
No more weird white rooms, no more maze of stairs and hallways. No more weird people insulting her for not knowing
things she had no way of knowing.

She walked further away. And further still, as though testing how far Shelley and Guy would let her go. She was pretty
sure she could outrun Shelley, with all her chains. But Guy had
a way of moving that suggested he was much faster than Charlene needed him to be.

"It won't work," Guy said from behind her. "But you'll
probably try anyway."

"I got a ten-er on it that she won't," Shelley said with a
jangle.

"I'll take that action," Guy said.

Charlene did her best to ignore them both. She was in
New York. She was almost home. She just needed to go the
rest of the way.

"It really won't work," Shelley said.

"Don't try to influence her," Guy responded.

"I'm just repeating what you said…"

Charlene couldn't take it anymore—she bolted.

She had never been that fast back on Earth. But that was
before, when she could feel the weight of her legs and the air in
her lungs. This Charlene had run to the end of the presentation
in the white room, and could have kept running indefinitely.

So Charlene ran with the confidence of a born athlete.
She headed south, away from the park, catching the corner

light just right to run across the street with a swarm of pushy pedestrians. She picked up speed as she broke away from the crowd, her summer flats somehow finding good purchase on the snowy sidewalk, her light blouse more than warm enough in the freezing air. She didn't question these things, or how she never ran into anyone or anything, instead focusing on pushing everything in her to keep moving forward, to get to home by any means necessary.

Charlene lived in Brooklyn, and that meant she'd have to take a bridge. She headed toward the Manhattan bridge, a vague mental image of the route she'd need to take guiding her toward Canal Street. She pushed herself faster, and the people she passed looked like blurs. But it didn't feel fast enough, so Charlene pushed herself faster still, until the blurs became streaks of color. She couldn't see individual buildings or people anymore, but it didn't matter. All that mattered was going home.

Charlene trusted whatever instinct in her was guiding her and put more speed into legs she could barely feel, until she couldn't see the streaks anymore, and everything around her faded into the grey darkness of a city night.

She felt like she could run forever.

"Well, that's ten I'm gonna miss," she heard Shelley say. The voice seemed to be behind her, as though she had never taken off, never ran, as though she was still where she started.

So she stopped.

She wasn't in Brooklyn. The houses around her were much too modern and large, sprawling monstrosities built to accommodate indoor-focused living. They were all painted variations on neutral shades, with repeating features of brick or stone in front to differentiate them. Here, the sky was clear, the manicured front lawns green and lush and free from snow. Here, the street was quiet and empty of people, oversized vehicles parked in driveways and on the street, shiny and clean or lightly covered in dust.

"I don't recognize this place," Shelley said.

"It's a suburb in California," Charlene said. She noticed then the neat string of Christmas lights that traced the outline of the nearest house, and recognized it as her Aunt Nancy's home. The lights weren't on as they were connected to a timer. None of the lights on the street would come on until it was the right time for them to do so, and all of them would turn off at the right time as well. Charlene was eight when she first heard the words "homeowners' association" and decided it was the most evil sounding thing she'd ever heard. The street looked pretty much the same as it did when she was a kid, and only the newness of the cars gave any sense of the passage of time.

"Huh," Guy said, coming up beside Charlene and into view. Somehow his suit and fedora looked even more out of place in the bright beige setting than they did in New York City. "This is what Christmas is for you? Central Park, and... this?"

Charlene nodded, finally putting the pieces together.

"I'm not really here, am I?" she asked quietly.

"No. This is just...a simulation," Guy said. "We give people a chance to visit their own Christmas history, help them get into the spirit. No pun intended."

No one laughed.

"Also, our house in New Jersey," Charlene said after a moment. "That is also what Christmas is for me. But every other year we came here, to my mom's family. Dad just had my uncle and grandpa left—so they came over on the other years. And then it was just Uncle Barry, and he moved in. He has learning disabilities and can't really live by himself. Gets confused about some things."

Charlene turned her back on her aunt's house—she wasn't particularly fond of the memories of being there—and walked down the street in the direction of a small community park that she always thought existed to somehow make up for the lack of backyards the houses had. How many times had she sought refuge there on too-warm Christmases?

"Is he here?" Charlene asked, hearing the drag of Shelley's chains as the other two followed her.

"Who?" Guy asked. He'd taken his jacket off and was dangling it behind his shoulder, and Charlene wondered why he didn't make it disappear the same way he'd made it appear.

"My grandfather," Charlene said. "He was always funny, and smelled like mint. He was exceedingly patient with me and my sister. Dad said that Grandpa Dickenson learned patience from Uncle Barry."

"No," Guy said gently. "Family members are never here."

Charlene nodded. That sounded right.

"I'm not sure I gave you the warning you needed," Shelley said, scraping and jangling into view. She stepped in front of Charlene, forcing her to stop and look at the greyish woman.

"You don't want to become like me."

"And how do I become like you?" Charlene said. She was annoyed by Shelly's intrusion, and could feel the frustration inside of her bubbling up and threatening to spill out.

"By refusing to let go," Shelley said, with more gentleness than Charlene expected. She lifted her arms—it looked painful to do so—and shook her chains, making the various steel books and shoes clatter together. "This isn't the stuff I held on to," she said. "It's just the stuff that made the chain. The things I held on to were less tangible, harder to turn into steel."

"Like what?"

"Family. Love. Memories. This is what happens. If you can't adjust to being here, if you can't accept your fate as a ghost, you'll get weighed down with symbols of your life. Literally. And for eternity."

Charlene wondered idly what items would make it to her chain. Coffee cups? Designer bags? Little collectibles from her favorite shows? Slippers?

"No one ever leaves this place? I spend the rest of time as a ghost? We all do?" Charlene wished she had the ability to huff, and envied Guy's deep sigh.

"Of course people leave this place. Just not…Marleys. She's trying to be kind to you."

Charlene ignored the feeling of guilt trying to work its way up her back and focused on the first part of what Guy said.

"So people leave. They can leave. How? Because I gotta tell you, Christmas isn't even my favorite holiday."

"They graduate," Guy said.

"Graduate?"

"Maybe evolve is the better word. The point is, they grow. Learn. Adapt. Change. And then somehow that makes them ready, and then they just…*leave*." There was something about the way he said the last word that made Charlene wonder if maybe he missed some of the other spirits who had left.

"One moment here, the next, gone," Shelley said, drawing Charlene's attention. She made a whoosh sound and pantomimed what Charlene presumed was a spirit zooming off into whatever came next.

"And no one knows why they do this, or where they go? It just happens?"

Shelley and Guy exchanged an unreadable look, piquing Charlene's frustration.

"Look, I just want to go home. That's all. I just want—"

"Don't say it," Shelley said, putting her hand out into a stop signal. "Please don't say it."

"You don't know what I was going to say," Charlene said, crossing her arms defensively.

"You want your life back," Shelley said. "Yeah, me too. Who doesn't? I had people. I had dreams. And I didn't want to let them go, either." She shook slightly, causing a clamoring commotion among her chains. "And now I never can."

Charlene uncrossed her arms, straightened her back, tried to do as many of the tricks as she could to calm herself down without the benefit of a working body to help her.

"I'm sorry," she said after a moment. "I know you're just

trying to help."

"To warn, honey," Shelley said. "Like a proper Marley should."

"Does this mean that now I'm going to be visited by three spirits?" Charlene said, forcing herself to smile.

"In a way," Guy said. "But only because shadowing spirits is the best way we figured out how to train new ones." He gestured at the houses around them, still large, still eerily quiet. "Can we take this discussion elsewhere? This place is giving me the creeps."

Charlene shrugged.

"I'm not really sure how we got here. I don't know how to leave. Can't you...do something?"

"This is your Christmas Portal, honey. Only you can guide us through it," Shelley said. "The Hall of Christmas Spirits is on the other side. But everyone has to work through their past a little first."

Charlene wondered why that was as she turned in a tight circle, looking all around and trying to figure out what a Christmas Portal was. There was so much she was missing! So many questions. But she had to admit that the quiet of the suburbs was getting to her too. So she closed her eyes, and focused. If this was a portal, then there had to be a door. And if there was a door, they could walk through it and get back to—wherever they were before. Charlene pictured the door. It was brown and wooden and looked an awful lot like the door to her apartment complex in Brooklyn. But she focused harder and imagined that this door would not open into her apartment, but into the

Hall of Christmas Spirits, whatever that was. She opened her eyes.

The door she had pictured was standing awkwardly, and alone, in the middle of the street.

"A bit literal, but not bad," Guy said. He gestured toward the door. "Lead the way."

Charlene walked to the door and opened it slowly, nervous about what she might see on the other side. Then she shoved it open with enthusiasm and triumph, showing a familiar gray hallway to the others.

Guy and Shelley exchanged a look that she couldn't interpret, dampening Charlene's sense of accomplishment.

"That's where you wanted to go, right?" she asked.

"It's as good a place as any," Guy said cryptically, and then walked through the door. Shelley shuffled in after, and Charlene had to wait a long moment for the last of her chain to cross over the threshold. A very long moment. A shockingly long moment, and Charlene wondered if Shelley's chain had grown somehow, maybe to make a point.

Finally, the last link was through the doorway, and Charlene looked up and down the street and tried to remember all the things she felt when she'd been in this place last. She hadn't always been miserable. She'd learned to ride a bike on this street, had roller skated with her sister and cousins. She'd twisted her ankle by that curb, and got treated like a princess by the other children, each taking turns waiting on her while she iced her ankle.

It was all so long ago.

"Coming?" Shelley asked from the other side of the door. Charlene turned and once again found herself staring at the other woman's chains. They had definitely left an impression.

So Charlene turned her back on her childhood memories, and stepped through the door.

CHAPTER SIX
Last Christmas

Charlene was losing track of locations again. Shelley had rambled off, but Guy had led Charlene down the hallway she had opened the Christmas Portal into. Garlands were draped across the tops of the walls and wreathes showing up every so many feet along the sides, and poinsettias taking up space on the floor between wreaths. There was the faint sound of music playing, which Charlene could just make out as an instrumental version of "What Child is This?" Eventually the hall opened up into a spectacularly large room, a giant Christmas tree in the middle of it that was so tall Charlene had to crane her neck to even get a glimpse of the glittering star at the top. Charlene could see no wire, but lights winked out at regular intervals, flickering like bright white candle flames. There were strange glass ornaments filled with swirling substances in silver, gold, red, green, blue, and purple nestled in among the branches and bows adorning the tree. Charlene pulled one closer to her for a better look, and the substance inside seemed to move faster, as though excited by her touch. It almost seemed to form a picture, and Charlene pulled it even closer to try to see what the picture could be.

"Please do be careful," Guy said, gently taking the ornament from her hand and releasing it so that it nestled softly back among the branches of the tree. "That's someone's Christmas memory—you wouldn't want to break it."

Charlene snatched her hand back.

"Whose memory?"

"Not sure. Best leave it alone."

He guided her around the tree, and Charlene saw that it was in the center of a room with mostly open arches all around the edges, each draped with lush green garlands that were in turn decorated with bright red bows. Every corner had poinsettias, and every archway center hung mistletoe. There were white lights lining the edges of the ceiling and dripping down like fake icicles, and sconces with actual candles sticking out of the stone walls, each sconce decorated with bows. While there were at least half a dozen arched doorways leading into the hall, only one was closed off with a tall, white pearlescent door. Charlene could have sworn the door was glowing, but Guy took her past it too quickly for her to ask about it.

He directed her toward a cluster of others—fellow ghosts, Charlene reminded herself—each wearing bright colors and with a glow of youth about them, regardless of their ages. They were chatting merrily, and were all smiles as Guy approached them.

"And how has it been?" he asked them with a smile.

A woman with a single, long, dark braid and a twinkle in her almond-shaped eyes gave him a slight nod, a familiarity. If Charlene had been able to feel her cheeks, she was sure they would have flushed with a pique of jealousy at the knowing look this woman gave her spirit trainer.

"Guy," the woman said, her voice low and rich, as though she spent her days smoking and singing. "It has been lovely to see you again. You have looked well."

Charlene tilted her head at the strange phrasing the woman used.

"Nomura, you also look well," Guy said back. "Are you going out again soon?"

"I have had an assignment," she said, looking past him at Charlene curiously.

"Up for a shadow?" he asked. Nomura looked from Charlene and then back at Guy, raising her eyebrows in question. "She's a quick learner," he added. "Feeling already."

Charlene smoothed her hands down over her pants, and nodded slightly. Nomura stepped forward. She was of a height with Charlene, but significantly leaner, a tight shirt showing off a flat stomach. Her eyes floated over Charlene's body, and Charlene was sure she was judging it, but the other woman's eyes stopped at Charlene's hands.

"You have had feeling already?" she asked.

"A little more all the time," Charlene responded. Nomura reached out her hand, and after a moment's hesitation, Charlene put out her own. Nomura's touch had heat in it as she took Charlene's hand, turning it around to look at the palm, turning it again to look at the top. And then with a single, sudden movement, she raised her own hand and slapped it down hard on top of Charlene's.

"Ow!" Charlene said, snatching her hand back and cradling it against her chest.

"And pain," Nomura said, and turned back to Guy. "She would have learned quickly."

It was hard to say if she was pleased by this or not.

"You'll take her then?" Guy asked.

"Wait, take me where?"

"To the past," Guy said. "Nomura is a Ghost of Christmas Past. I'm surprised you didn't notice."

"I would have taken her," Nomura said with a formal nod of her head. "She would have gone with me." She looked at Charlene expectantly.

Charlene wanted to say no, wanted to stay with Guy. But she also had to learn how to be a Christmas Spirit, or else end up like poor Shelley, stuck in chains. So she lifted her chin and looked squarely at Nomura.

"I'm ready when you are," she said. Nomura smiled back.

"We would have been going, then," she said. She turned to walk away, the other Ghosts of Christmas Pasts moving out of her way and giving Charlene smiles of encouragement. As she passed through the group, Charlene tried to imagine herself as one of them. They just looked like people—strong looking, bright eyed people.

"We would have wished you luck!" a man said as she passed. She smiled back, and gave him a little wave.

Nomura moved quickly, and Charlene hurried to keep up with her, following her down another hallway, and to another door.

"We have not needed doors, but you have had to need them, so a door it has been." The door opened, and only then did Charlene notice that there was no handle on it. Nomura walked through and Charlene followed, curious.

The room started off looking normal enough, with walls and a floor, but then it faded into a white light. Not that there was a white light at the end of the room, but that the room itself seemed to dissolve into the white light. It looked similar to the room the welcoming presentation was in, and Charlene hoped that this one wouldn't also have scrolling words in it. Nomura stopped just short of the edge of the floor, and Charlene took position next to her.

"It wouldn't have been long," Nomura said.

So Charlene waited. She had tons of questions, but couldn't figure out how to start asking them. She wasn't sure Nomura would want to answer them. She also wasn't sure she would be able to work through all the tenses to figure out what Nomura was really saying.

True to Nomura's word though, Charlene didn't have to wait long for something to happen. There was a sound coming from the white light, and just as Charlene was starting to figure out what it was, her eyes confirmed it: a Marley was shuffling through the light and into the room with Nomura and Charlene.

The Marley was androgynous, with short hair and gender-neutral clothing, and Charlene revamped her use of pronouns to reflect that. The Marley looked very young, and their eyes were filled with sadness, their steps particularly heavy and dragging.

"Would it have been an unusually hard visit, Jeri?" Nomura asked gently. Jeri nodded, their chains rattling mournfully.

"My cousin," they said. "He struggled so much, even when I was alive. It wasn't much better, now. You have your work cut out for you."

"We would have done our best," Nomura said, patting Jeri gently on the back as they passed. Charlene gave them a nod of encouragement and got a sad smile in return.

"New?" Jeri asked.

"First time," Charlene responded.

"Good luck," Jeri said. "And try not to get too caught up in it all. Remember, you can't actually change the past."

With that, Jeri shuffled out the door, not seeming to much notice or care where they were going. Charlene felt the weight of Nomura's hand on her shoulder, and turned back toward her, and the white light.

"It would have been our turn," she said. Her grip was much tighter than Charlene would have thought. "I would have had to keep hold. You would have stayed close."

Charlene nodded agreement. They walked forward into the light together.

For a moment, there was just the white light, so thick and bright that Charlene couldn't see Nomura. But she felt the grip of the ghost's hand on her shoulder, which kept her steady. Then the white light dissolved into shapes: a dresser, a desk, a bed. Nomura stopped their forward walk when the space around them became a clearly defined bedroom with a single figure sprawled out on top of the covers, staring at the ceiling. Nomura took her hand off Charlene's shoulder then. Her clothes had changed during her trip in the light and she was wearing a lightweight white dress, her hair piled on top of her head and entwined with white lights and sparkling beads, making it almost look like parts of her hair were on fire.

"He won't be able to see you," Nomura said. "Or me, until I want him to."

"Wait, your words…"

"When we're back on Earth, we can speak normally," Nomura said. "There's something about…where we were before…that changes our speech. I say things the way I'm saying them now. But they come out the way you heard it. I don't know why. One of those mysteries, I guess."

"Because you're a Ghost of Christmas Past, you can only speak in—what was that? Past perfect?"

"A bastardation of it, anyway," Nomura said. "Apparently simple past would have been too easy." She winced at her use of "would have".

"And if I become a Past Ghost…"

"It will happen to you too," Nomura said. "It's not that bad though, really. Being from the past gives you sort of a youthful glow. My arms never looked like this when I was alive—but you have to have a strong grip. All the ghosts do. Are you ready?"

"What are you going to do?"

"There's a bit of a script," Nomura said. "And then some travel. Really nothing to it."

Nomura stepped forward, glancing at the digital clock on the man's bedside table. It read 12:59. Then the red digits changed to 01:00 A.M. Charlene couldn't see Nomura doing anything in particular, but the man on the bed seemed to suddenly notice her.

"Oh shit! Another one! You're the one, right? The one my cousin warned me about?"

"I am," Nomura said her voice low and strong.

"Who and what are you?"

"I am the Ghost of Christmas Past," Nomura said.

"Shit shit shit shit," the man said in return, pulling on his hair and practically rocking back and forth. "Why me? Why are you here?"

"I am here for your welfare," Nomura said, and then looking at the confused look on the man's face, added, "to help you be better."

"That's what Jeri said. They said that they were here to warn me, that three spirits would visit me." He was shaking, and Charlene couldn't help but feel sorry for him. As hard as it was to be on her side of this, it seemed like it actually might be harder to be on the other. She wondered how she would have felt if she were visited by ghosts instead of becoming one.

"This is so unreal," the man said, getting up and pacing around. "What the hell did I smoke?"

Charlene noticed a large bong next to his bed and glanced up at Nomura, who very discreetly glanced at Charlene with a look of annoyance.

"I am not a hallucination," Nomura said firmly. "I am here to show you your past."

"Oh shit oh shit oh shit," the man said, sitting back on the bed, head in hands.

Nomura gave Charlene an exasperated look, and Charlene

shrugged back in sympathy. This didn't seem to be going the way Nomura hoped.

"He really can't see me?" Charlene asked. Nomura shook her head slightly. "Or hear me?" Nomura shook her head again.

"Hey!" Charlene shouted. The man didn't move, but kept up his litany of cursing and rocking. Nomura stifled a giggle.

Charlene took the opportunity to look around the room, taking in details to try to get a sense of where—and when—she was. There wasn't much in the space except clothes and wrinkled sheets. The man didn't have art up on the walls, and the top of his dresser was a mess of personal products. Charlene turned around and wasn't surprised that the white light was gone. Instead she saw the rest of the room, including a chair overflowing with towels and other laundry, and the bedroom door. Charlene glanced at Nomura, who had taken a few steps toward the man.

"I am here to help you," Nomura said to the man, still firmly but not as loudly as before.

Charlene took her opportunity and dashed through the bedroom door and into the rest of the apartment.

There wasn't much more to see. One bathroom, very dirty and with way too many pairs of underwear on the floor, a hallway that hadn't been vacuumed in a very long time, and a small living room and kitchen area separated by a large island, high enough on the living room side to have two bar stools tucked up close to it. Charlene wandered over to a window and looked out. Wherever she was, it was a place that got a lot of snow. She was looking out at other apartment buildings across an alley, and when she twisted to the right, she could just about make out a street at the end of the alley. She turned back around looked at the various items on the coffee table, peeking through take out containers to see if there was anything else of interest there. She spotted a piece of mail, and squinted at the partially stained envelope, reading the address label: Brody Higgins, who lived in Chicago, Il, in zip code 60609.

Charlene became very still. She knew that zip code. She had sent packages to that zip code. Her older sister Emily lived in that zip code.

Charlene didn't even think—she just headed for the front door of the apartment. Her hand went through the door handle when she tried to open it, but that only made Charlene hesitate for a moment. Then she walked through the door. She thought she might see something—wood grain or something—but it was just a moment of darkness, and then a return to the light.

She stopped on the other side to look behind her and wonder at what she had just done. Denial my ass, she thought. She was getting the hang of this ghost thing.

She went down the nearest stairwell with new determination and confidence. She had to pass through two more doors to get outside, and then she was on a street, turning from one direction to the other to try to figure out where to go next.

No one had told her what it meant to go to Earth, what the rules were. In fact, no one had really told her anything.

"I'm a ghost," she said out loud. "What can ghosts do?"

She started walking and watched as her footsteps fell through thick banks of snow, which was a good thing, since she definitely didn't have the shoes for this kind of weather. When her foot fell through a previously unspotted pile of dog poop, she jumped back, landing in a snowbank that went up to her knees.

She jumped out of that as quickly as she could, trying to find some part of the street that made her feel that she was walking on it instead of through it. As she struggled to find a part of the street that didn't cover her feet, it occurred to her to wonder how she was standing on the street at all—what was holding her up?

Uncomfortable with that idea, she came up with another one and looked up. It was a ridiculous idea. But then, everything had been ridiculous lately.

Charlene jumped into the air. She landed lightly, her feet barely registering the sense of ground beneath her.

"Landing is for mortals," she chided herself. "I. Am. A. Ghost."

She closed her eyes and jumped again, willing herself to stay in the air this time. When she didn't feel anything, she opened her eyes and looked down. She was hovering slightly above the ground.

It was a scarier sight than she thought it would be, and she let out an involuntary squeal, pinwheeling her arms to keep balance that she didn't need to keep. Her feet wobbled and dipped for a moment, and she focused hard, stabilizing herself in her hover position above the ground.

"Good job, ghost," she said, grinning. "Now, higher." She looked up and focused, putting all her energy into the feeling of *up*. She floated a few inches higher, waving her arms around to keep her balance.

"You got this," she told herself, keeping her arms steady. "And up again." This time her rise was smoother, more stable, and soon she was floating up above the apartment building she had just come out of. At this point she put her effort into stopping, until she was dangling in the air. She tried not to look at the distance beneath her, tried to remind herself that as a ghost she not only had nothing to fear from falling, that she was, in fact, capable of flying.

It seemed to work.

All she had to do next was float to her sister's house—and hope her sister was home.

Only she didn't know Chicago that well from the ground, and she didn't have any better sense of it from six stories up. Charlene spun slowly in a circle, trying to think of which direction to head in. Did ghosts need a sense of direction?

She closed her eyes and thought of her sister. Emily was three years older and four decades more cynical. She had a sardonic sense of humor that had caused their parents no shortage of problems when she and Charlene were younger, and had made her particularly popular among certain peers. She was bitingly witty, and Charlene both loathed and adored her for it—adored it when it was aimed at Charlene's enemies and loathed it when it was aimed at her.

Somewhere along the way, the loathing eked out the adoration, and Charlene hadn't really talked to Emily much in the past few years. They talked on holidays and birthdays, and now and then when their parents were being spectacularly annoying and they needed to vent. But their lives were very different. Emily lived in Chicago with her husband and twin three-year olds, and most of her conversation was about fellow moms that Charlene had never met. Charlene had less and less to contribute, and felt silly trying to talk about the problems of her single life and stagnant career.

But that was before she died. Now, all Charlene could think about was how much she missed her sister. So she pictured her—her light brown hair cut mom-short since the twins were born, with a streak of blue in it to remind her that she wasn't just a mom. Her eyes crinkled in the corners when she laughed, which was often. Her nose was permanently freckled from their vacations in California. She had a scar over her left eyebrow from a piercing gone bad.

All Charlene wanted was to see her sister's face again. And maybe, if she just focused…

Charlene's ears picked up on the voices while her eyes were still closed—little, high-pitched voices. Charlene opened her eyes to see her niece and nephew bent over a stack of blocks, Cara telling Damien which block to put where. He was dutifully listening, stacking his blocks very carefully.

"Hi guys!" Charlene exclaimed, running forward to try to hug the twins. Her hands went through their little bodies, and her voice was lost to their ears.

"Stack it like this," Cara said, demonstrating the proper technique to her brother. Charlene pulled back, sitting low on her heels to put herself more on the same level as the little ones.

"Like this?" Damien asked, his block precariously balancing on top of another.

"Yeah," Cara said. "That looks good."

"You can't hear me, can you?" Charlene asked, already knowing the answer. Damien's next attempt to stack a block toppled the tower he'd been working on, and Cara put her little hands on her hips.

"You have to stack better!" she said. "We're building castles."

She seemed to have her mother's way of bossing people around. Charlene smiled.

"You two doing okay?" a voice said from over Charlene's shoulder, and she turned to see her sister peeking into the room. Emily's hair was longer than Charlene remembered, the blue all but faded out.

"We're building castles," Damien said.

"Trying to," Cara added, still clearly annoyed.

"Okay, but this is your ten minute warning. Dinner soon."

Emily saw whatever she needed to in her children's faces, and then kept moving down the hall. Charlene followed her into a living room that sported a large Christmas tree speckled in fake white frost and covered in homemade decorations, and lots of toys scattered around and clearly abandoned in the middle of play. Emily bent down to pick things up as she went, dumping them into a plastic bin by the wall.

"Is this now?" Charlene asked. "It was July. Is this after I died? Before?"

She didn't expect her sister to answer.

"After," a familiar voice said instead. Charlene whirled to see Guy leaning against the fireplace mantel, his hat held loosely in his hand, his jacket nowhere to be seen, forearms exposed and flexing. "And you're not supposed to be here."

"So, I'm dead? I'm seeing my sister after I died? That explains how grown the twins looked." Charlene turned her back on Guy and continued to follow her sister into the kitchen, where Emily was pouring a glass of wine. She watched her sister take a long sip, and then a deep breath, and then another long sip before putting the glass down.

"Do you even care that you're in trouble?" Guy said, coming around the corner.

"She needs a haircut," Charlene said. "She never needs a haircut. She's always so good about that."

"She's had a rough year," Guy said. "Her sister died over the summer."

Emily pulled a tray of chicken nuggets from the oven, and another one of fries.

"She looks so sad," Charlene said. "That can't just be about me."

"I get it. I get coming here, trying to see her. Honestly, I'm a little impressed that you made it this far. It usually takes so much longer for spirits to muck things up like this."

"Can I talk to her? There has to be a way, right? I can tell her I'm okay. I can tell her not to be so sad. If Nomura can talk to whatshisname, I can talk to Emily, right? There's a way, I just know it."

Charlene focused—she had walked through doors, she

had flown, she had transported—what was a little speech compared to all that?

"Emily, I—"

But Emily was no longer in front of her. Instead she was staring at the Christmas tree in the Hall of Christmas Spirits, Guy blocking most of her view of the tree.

"No," he said. "You don't get to do that."

"Why?" Charlene asked, suddenly angry. "It would have worked. I know it would have!"

"There's a good chance, yes," Guy said. "But you still don't get to do that."

"Because I'm a ghost?"

"Because it's cruel."

Before Charlene could respond, she felt a hand clamp down on her shoulder and turned to find a glaring Nomura.

"How would you have dared!" She yanked her hand away, and took a step forward, getting up in Charlene's face. "I would have trusted you. You would have disappointed me. You…" She couldn't seem to find the right words. Instead she stepped back and turned on Guy.

"No," she said. And again, with even more force: "no!"

Then she spun on her heel and walked away so fast she seemed to glide.

Guy looked at Charlene and shook his head.

"Strike one," he said sadly. "The past doesn't want you. Let's try the present."

CHAPTER SEVEN
A Holly Jolly Christmas

"Exactly what rule did I break?" Charlene asked as she followed Guy down yet another hallway toward yet another door decorated with a huge wreath covered in pine cones coated in silver glitter. She could hear music again, this time an enthusiastic child's choir singing about Rudolf the Red Nosed Reindeer.

"Come on now, don't pretend ignorance," Guy said back over his shoulder. The door opened before him without use of a door handle, something Charlene was starting to understand was normal for this place.

"It's not my fault we ended up in Chicago," Charlene tried again. She wasn't really sure why she was trying so hard to justify her actions. "I mean, if you ended up in the same place as your family member, wouldn't you want to try?"

Guy ignored her and kept walking, turning sharply to walk through yet another self-opening door, with another spectacularly gaudy wreath on it, this one in blue and purple. Charlene followed at a trot. Whatever his feelings, it was making his normally brisk pace even quicker. So she wasn't prepared for him to stop suddenly, and had to put out her hands to keep herself from running into him. She was shocked by the feel of his body, her hands pressed against his back. He was warm. She didn't know why she assumed he wouldn't be, but he was, and she pulled her hands back quickly, suddenly embarrassed to have touched him.

He moved aside, and Charlene avoided looking at his face, not sure she wanted to see his expression. Instead she looked past him, where a group of people sat around what looked like a large, silvery pool. Most of the light in the room seemed to be coming from the pool itself, giving everyone a slightly eerie under lit look. They were very focused on whatever they could see inside the silver. The pool itself was fed by a waterfall of the same substance that seemed to come in from the ceiling, and a small river trickled out of it and toward another smaller pool to the side, from which yet another stream of silver trickled toward what looked like a hole in the floor, where Charlene couldn't track its path anymore.

"Can I have some attention, please?" Guy asked. He was hatless and jacket-less and while he showed no sign of effort from his near-sprint through the Hall of Christmas Spirits, Charlene still felt that Guy looked slightly warm, as though he was barely containing the heat of his temper.

"You're up, Cary," a woman said, and as she spoke, her hair seemed to get longer, then shorter, then longer.

"I suppose," Cary said in return, his facial hair growing and then receding, and then growing again. It made him almost harder to look at than Walzer was. "But isn't this the one who is pissing off Nomura?"

"First timer, still fresh. Had the bad luck of getting a Scrooge who lived in the same place as her still living sister," Guy said. "You remember how it is."

Charlene felt this was kinder than she deserved, and kinder than she expected Guy to offer her.

Cary looked Charlene over, and then shrugged. As she watched, his clothes began to change as well, his shirt going from a light grey to a bright salmon, and then changing to a deep blue. The sleeves and collar seemed to change with the color.

"Keeping up with current fashion," Guy told her. "The present is always moving and changing."

The first woman who spoke was even harder to look at, as her makeup seemed to be in a state of constant flux: a natural look, then a stylized look, shine and gloss appearing and disappearing.

"How fast is time going?" Charlene asked. "I just got here, but already it was Christmas—six months later. And the rate that they are changing at…."

"Is she watching the presentation?" Cary asked.

"She ran through it," Guy said back, adjusting the hat that suddenly appeared on his head and avoiding Cary's gaze. Charlene wondered if the hat was connected to Guy's feelings in some way, or if he just wanted a touch more style amongst the Ghosts of Christmas Presents' constant changing. "But I assure you, she is ready for the field. Just needs a good guide."

Cary eyed Charlene suspiciously.

"She isn't even aware of how time works here," he said. "And then what she is doing with Nomura…."

"A mistake," Charlene said. "That I promise won't happen again. Just so long as I don't go back to Chicago. Or New York.

Or New Jersey. Or maybe California."

Guy gave her an exasperated look from under his hat.

"Not helping," he said under his breath.

"As if where we are actually matters," Cary said, standing up and walking toward Charlene. "Come along."

Charlene gave Guy an apologetic shrug and followed after Cary, watching as the length of the Ghost of Christmas Present's pants and height of his socks changed. Ankles were in. Ankles were out. Ankles were in again. Charlene had to wonder at the speed of fashion trends.

"There is one rule," Cary said. "Stay with me." He stopped at the second, smaller pool at the edge of the room and reached out a hand. Charlene took it, unsurprised by the strength of his grip. All the ghosts seemed to have strong grips.

"And here we go," Cary said, jumping into the pool, bringing Charlene in with him.

The substance wasn't wet, per se, but it did move like water around Charlene. She wondered for a moment how she was going to breathe until she remembered that she didn't have to. Still, she felt like she was submerged for a very long time, being pulled along by a current and Cary's strong hold. Finally, she felt herself being pulled out of the silvery substance and into a room. Once she was standing, Cary let go of her hand, and Charlene looked around. This room was very different than the last room she visited, large and with a high bed made up with rich linens and lots of decorative pillows. There were multiple doors in the walls, and Charlene could peek through one to see that it was a closet, and another to see that it led to a bathroom that looked larger than her entire Brooklyn apartment. The last door was closed, and as she watched, the door knob turned, hesitantly, as though the person on the other side was unsure. Charlene looked over at Cary, whose outfit had changed again, becoming a deep green robe over dark gray pants, with slippers to match the robe. The robe peeked slightly open, revealing a bare and well-chiseled chest. He had a crown of holly on his head, and Charlene tried not to stare.

"Come in," Cary said to whoever was on the other side of the closed door. "Come in and know me better, woman!"

The door swung open cautiously, and a woman wearing a matching set of pajama tops and bottoms in pink and grey plaid and a flowy pink robe peeked around the doorframe, staring at wonder at the room.

"It's my bedroom!" she said, then turned around to see another version of the same room behind her.

"I am the Ghost of Christmas Present," Cary said. "Look upon me!"

The woman did as she was told, stepping fully into the room.

"I can't believe this is still happening," the woman said. "I feel like I've already learned so much. I'm really not sure how much more I can take."

"Oh, well, then I guess I'll be going," Cary said, shrugging.

"Wait!" The woman stepped closer to Cary, reaching out to him. "I can go on. I really can. I want to see what you will show me."

"Then touch my robe," Cary told her, catching Charlene's

eye as well. She assumed the order was as much for her as for the woman in pajamas. She reached out dutifully. The robe was soft and thick and easy to hold on to.

Suddenly, the scene in front of them shifted, as though they were on a conveyor belt and passing through different rooms. There were people shopping, and others clearing snow from sidewalks, and others putting decorations on trees. Finally, the scene in front of them settled into that of a group of people standing outside a church.

"We have to go in," a girl was saying to another woman who looked an awful lot like the woman in the pajamas, just thinner and maybe slightly younger.

"Your aunt Valerie will be here," the woman said back. "Just go on in. I'm sure she'll be joining us shortly." She made a shooing gesture at the girl, who shrugged and pulled open a heavy wooden door to go inside.

"Oh now," the pajama woman said, who Charlene assumed was the missing Valerie. "I told Melinda I might come. *Might.* I certainly didn't mean to make her wait, or miss out on anything."

"She's not going to wait much longer," Cary said confidently. "And we shall see what you might be missing."

After a moment, and with one last look at the screen of her phone for any missed message, Melinda sighed deeply and pulled open the door and went inside. The door, heavy as it was, took its time closing, and Cary, Valerie, and Charlene just made it inside before it did.

They followed Melinda down an aisle and into a pew

crowded with people who all seemed to be related to her. Cary and Valerie slid into the pew behind them, filling up the only gap left in several feet in either direction. Charlene stood awkwardly in the aisle.

"We're not going to stay for the whole thing, are we?" she asked Cary. He shot her a side-eye that was filled with disgust, and settled himself more comfortably into his seat. Everyone around him was dressed up in their Christmas best, but somehow his pajamas didn't seem to look as awkward as Valerie's.

"Oh, I'm so glad I'm not actually going to miss the service!" Valerie said.

Charlene looked around some more for another place to sit and found a small square of bench just across the aisle from Cary and Valerie. She sat gingerly, trying not to get too close to the people next to her as she didn't want to watch their thighs go into hers.

Then, a large man started making his way down the pew toward where she was sitting. Charlene watched him with growing alarm until he was directly in front of her, his ass in front of her face. Then his ass was moving toward her face, and all the rest of her, and she shot up so fast she accidentally floated up above the pews.

She saw Cary glare up at her and make a small motion for her to come down. Charlene looked around for a good place to do so, one that wouldn't have her landing on anyone or anything, and she drifted off to the side in her search. She could see Cary gesture more dramatically, and ignored him.

It wasn't like she was doing this on purpose. The church

was very crowded, and having one unwanted bottom move toward her face was more than enough for Charlene. She finally spotted a relatively clear spot in the back right of the church and floated to it, willing herself to land lightly on the stone floor. Somehow she overshot, sinking waist deep into it, and looked around in a panic for something to grab on to so she could pull herself back up. She saw a large candle stand and reached for it, watching her hand pass through the heavy metal legs.

Right, she thought. Ghost. Pulling herself up wasn't going to work. She thought about jumping, but something about only being able to see half her body made it harder to picture that. How does one jump without legs? Since she couldn't figure out how to move up, and certainly didn't want to move any further down, there was only one other direction she could think about going—forward. So she focused on that, propelling herself forward through sheer will. Finally, she came to the back wall of the church, and then there was a moment of darkness as she passed through it, and then she was on the other side.

As the main room of the church had been up some stairs, Charlene only had to float forward a little more to have her feet more or less touching the ground again. Once they did, she turned around to walk back toward the church door.

She stopped when she spotted Guy, leaning back on the steps, jacket and hat nowhere to be seen. He looked impossibly casual, and particularly attractive.

"One rule, just the one," he said.

"This wasn't my fault!" Charlene said. "I didn't try to leave! I was trying to find a place to sit. But then there was a large ass coming at me, and then I was in the air. I didn't even mean to. And then I tried to come down, and I missed, and then I kept going to try to get back to normal ground again. I had every intention of staying, I really did!"

"Ghosts of Christmas Present aren't known for their patience," Guy said, standing up in one fluid motion. "Cary especially."

"Is he going to stay to watch the whole service?" Charlene asked. "Can't I just meet him after?"

"Sorry doll, he already sent the signal. It's why I'm here."

Charlene looked around. She tried to get her bearings, get a sense of where she was. Since she had already messed up her shadowing mission, she thought she might make a go of it, see if she could see her parents, or Jonelle, or anyone else she knew.

"Charlotte, North Carolina," Guy said. "You don't know anyone here."

"But I went from New York to California in almost no time," Charlene said.

"That was a simulation," Guy countered.

"Was it?" She met his gaze squarely, trying to see if he was telling the truth. Instead, she was newly reminded just how gorgeous his eyes were, and looked away. "But this is Earth. And I could…."

"Break the rules again?" Guy walked smoothly to Charlene, offering her his arm. "You ran through the presentation, skipped out on Nomura to visit your sister, and flew away from Cary. Maybe quit while you're behind."

Charlene crossed her arms across her body, shivering

slightly.

"Are you...cold?" Guy asked, disbelief evident in his voice.

"You say that like it's a bad thing," Charlene said. Guy shook his head in response and pulled his jacket out of thin air, and put it around Charlene's shoulders. She pulled it tightly around herself and smiled up at him. "Thanks," she said. "But aren't we just going back to the Hall of Christmas Spirits?"

"Eventually," he said, offering her his arm again. This time she took it, and he led her away from the church, down a tree-lined sidewalk, the trees dusted in snow. "It occurs to me that from your perspective, all of this is happening very quickly. And that there is a lot you don't know."

"Like why time seems to be moving so quickly, or what the Hall of Christmas Spirits actually is and why it has so many hallways, or how come Marleys can only visit people they know, or why the Christmas tree had ornaments full of memories, or why everyone is unhappy when they learn that I can feel things, or how come your hat and coat just appear and disappear." Charlene took a breath. "I feel like I don't know anything."

"So ask me," Guy said. "One thing at a time though— even I can't keep up with all of that."

Charlene sorted through all her questions. But the most pressing one, the one she hadn't really thought to ask until just then, was walking beside her.

"Who are you?" she asked. "You're not a Ghost of Christmas Past, Present, or Future, and you're not a Trip, and you're not a Marley. You just...show up. How? Why? What role do you actually play here?"

"I'm your trainer," Guy said, his voice even. "I go where I need to go, to help you."

"But you were alive once, like me? So you're also a ghost?"

"I prefer spirit, but yes."

Charlene let her mind wander for a moment, trying to think of the next thing to ask while also enjoying the closeness of Guy's body.

"When were you born?" she asked.

"That's not what you really want to know," he countered. "You want to know when I died. And how. And maybe why I haven't moved on, if moving on is actually possible."

Charlene nodded. He was right, she did want to know all of that. He stopped and turned her toward him, leaving her hand still on his arm. She had to fight the urge to slide it up to his shoulder, and willed herself to be very still while also enjoying the heat of his touch.

"I wish I could make this easier for you," he said. "But there is only so much I can teach you. There is only so much I'm allowed to tell you." He pulled her closer then, leaning his face down very close to hers and speaking very softly, his voice deep and warm. "But I think you will figure it out. You have already advanced so much, so quickly. Just give yourself time."

Charlene stared up at him, wishing her sense of smell was back so that she could take in his scent, and wishing also that he would wrap an arm around her the way he did his jacket, pull her even closer. Instead he let her go, stepping back with a sad smile.

"I think maybe you need a break from the visits," he said. Then he held up one hand and waited while Charlene focused in on it. He snapped his fingers, and everything around them disappeared.

CHAPTER EIGHT
Silent Night

Charlene was back in her room in the Hall of Christmas Spirits, staring at the little tree carved into the headboard of the little bed inside it. She wasn't sure why that was where Guy sent her, but she was glad to see something familiar. She would have rather been back on that street in North Carolina, Guy's jacket around her shoulders, his body close to hers. But she supposed that was more than she deserved after ruining her chances to become a Ghost of Christmas Past or Present.

Someone had put the bedding on her bed since last she was in the room. The blankets and pillow cases were, of course, in Christmas colors, red and green plaid with thick, red satin edging, and she flopped down on top of them, staring up at a stone ceiling. Nothing was making sense.

"Just let it go," she said to herself. That had been the advice she failed to take when she followed Stephen, however long ago that was. It felt like a lifetime ago. She laughed bitterly. It had been a lifetime ago—it had been when she was alive.

But she couldn't. She couldn't let it go, and she followed him anyway, and then she spilled her coffee, and then a tree fell on her and she died. She literally was stuck in this nightmare of an afterlife because she couldn't let something go. And what lesson did she learn from that?

None, apparently, since she continued to muck things up in the afterlife, going to see Emily, floating in church. She giggled at that second one, remembering what it was like to be above all those people as they stared solemnly ahead, waiting for the service to begin.

A knock on the door broke the image for her, and Charlene propped herself up on her elbows and stared at it warily.

"Hello?" she called out.

"It's Shelley," a voice from the other side said. "Can I come in?"

"Sure," Charlene said, sitting up properly as the door swung open and Shelley shuffled in. Charlene watched as Shelley pulled out the chair by the desk opposite her and then worked to arrange her chains around her so that she could sit. It was an awkward and noisy affair, made harder by her skirt and hat, both of which got twisted up in chains twice and had to be set right, and Shelley worked hard to get her chain situated so that she could sit down without sitting on anything pointy or bumpy.

"Just about got it," she said at last, sitting down tentatively at first, and then more solidly, grinning at Charlene. "Just takes a bit of adjustment."

"Yeah," Charlene said, noncommittedly.

"So, I heard you're having a hard time, honey," Shelley said, her hands resting on a pair of steel heels that had ended up on her lap.

"A bit," Charlene admitted. "Sort of blew both Christmas Past and Christmas Present," she said. "Makes me think maybe

I should have watched the full orientation presentation."

"Oh, that thing?" Shelley made a dismissive motion with her hand, chain links dangling from her wrist like a very thick bracelet. "A bunch of scrolling words can't really prepare anyone for all of, well, this." She gestured at the room and then at herself. "It's a lot to take in, and if it's any consolation, I think you're doing real swell, honey. You're picking up on things so fast! You're doing way better than I ever did."

Charlene didn't want to say, but she hoped so. Her entire goal was to heed Shelley's warning and not become a Marley like her.

"That's nice of you to say," she said instead. "But I only have one chance left to…" She faltered.

"Avoid my fate? It's okay, you can say it. I don't want you to become a Marley anymore than you want to."

"Can I ask," Charlene began, unsure how to continue.

"How it happened? Like, what went wrong?"

Charlene nodded.

Shelley adjusted her seat, working around her chain so that she could cross one leg over the other, twisting around so she could rest her arm on the back of the desk chair.

"It's not that something went wrong," she said. "It's more that I was having a hard time giving up being human. It was little things, like wanting to eat, or use door knobs, or take a bath. I even asked for a change of clothes."

"You can do that?" Charlene said, looking down at the same stained blouse and pants she'd been wearing when she died.

"Oh yeah! Someone should have told you that. You can wear anything you wore in life, if you want to, for a little bit at least. Why don't you try? It will be good practice." She smiled and waited expectantly.

"How do I do it?" Charlene asked.

"Same as any of the other things I heard you've done, like flying. That had to be a hoot! I never got to fly before, and you really can't with all this." She gestured at herself. "Go on! Change your clothes!"

Charlene nodded and sat up straighter, first tying to think about what she would rather be wearing. It was hard to think of something good with Shelley, all dolled up like she just walked off the set of *His Girl Friday* sitting next to her. She didn't think she wanted to try anything like that. For one, she wasn't sure she could imagine the proper foundational garments for it. For two, she never wore that in life, so she probably couldn't even if she tried.

Instead, Charlene tried to think about a time when she thought she looked pretty, and comfortable in her own skin. Maybe it was because of all the decorations around her, but the first thing that came to mind was an outfit she wore to a Christmas party Jonelle threw the year before Charlene died. Charlene had worn dark blue boot-cut jeans over a pair of thick-heeled brown ankle boots, a lightly sequined green spaghetti strapped tank top, and a cream-colored three-quarter sleeve blazer over it. She'd worn silver hoops that Jonelle had given her the year before, and her hair was down and curled into waves for the occasion. She'd gotten lots of compliments that night, and had been able to graciously accept them. It was a good memory, and as good an outfit as any.

Charlene focused on the outfit, how it looked, how it fit, and how it felt. Then she opened her eyes and looked down. Everything was exactly as she remembered, and she grinned, standing up to twirl and get the full effect, stepping over the ends of Shelley's chain to do so.

"Nice!" Shelley said. "Not a dress, but still, a might better than what you've been sporting."

"I've always preferred pants," Charlene said. "I don't have to worry about how to sit in them."

Shelley laughed at her.

"Whatever floats your boat, honey," she said. "You're catching on real quick to these ghost tricks. That's all you need. Embrace the spirit, and leave the rest behind."

Charlene sat on her bed again, and kicked at part of Shelley's chain with the toe of her boot.

"Is it very heavy?" she asked.

"You get used to it," Shelley said. "Why, you wanna try it?"

"Could I?"

Shelley shrugged.

"Sure. It may be just the motivation you need." She worked more of the chain off her shoulder, piling a fair amount of it on the floor in front of Charlene. Considering that the woman herself wasn't altogether solid, Shelley's chain had a hefty mass when Charlene bent to pick it up. She wrapped a coil around her arm to get the feel of it. The parts that touched her skin felt cold.

"So you still feel?" she asked.

"I feel enough," Shelley said. Charlene caught the way that Shelley was looking at the links wrapped around her arm, and let them slide gently off and back on to the floor.

"I'm sorry this happened to you," she said.

"Not your fault, honey," Shelley said. "Just the way the cookie crumbles, I guess." She stood up then, gathering coils of chain around her to minimize any dangling bits. "But I should let you rest. If you need rest."

It was another noisy production for Shelley to get herself out of Charlene's door—the room really wasn't big enough for Shelley and her chain—and then she turned back before closing it behind her.

"But maybe you should try to not rest," she said. "Ghosts don't need sleep. Or beds. Or rooms. So maybe, if you can, you can try to figure out more ways to be ghost-like." She smiled sadly at Charlene. "Not like me."

Charlene nodded.

"I really appreciate you coming by."

"Sure thing, honey," Shelley said. Then she closed the door.

Charlene stared around the little cell-like room. She realized that it wouldn't take much to imagine books on the shelves, or trinkets. Maybe, if she was very good, even framed photos. But that felt too human. She looked over at the gray curtain and remembered how she was able to make a view past it, and wondered what other views she could make. Was that being ghost-like or human-like? She smoothed her hand over the blanket, taking in the texture. That was probably a human thing, she realized. Feeling was a human thing. She needed to do ghost things.

Charlene stood up and walked to the door, reaching automatically for the handle before stopping herself. Ghosts didn't need handles. Instead she straightened her spine, put her chin up, and walked through the solid-looking wood.

Instead of ending up in the grey hallway, like she expected, Charlene found herself staring at the large Christmas tree in the Hall instead. She looked over her shoulder, but there was no door behind her. She had wanted to go to the hall, so now she was in the hall. She realized then why Guy had said it didn't matter how many hallways he took her down—she could always go back to her little room. She just had to picture herself going there.

Pleased with this discovery, Charlene wandered around the tree, taking note again of the unusual white door. She wondered what was behind it and moved closer to investigate when she spotted a cluster of Ghosts of Christmas Past. She swiftly turned around and headed the other way, looking for a quick exit. Maybe because she needed one, she spotted another wooden door where she was sure there wasn't one before, and dashed through it.

Charlene was back in what she had come to think of as the Holiday Spirit Break Room. It was strange to see a place not completely wrapped up in garland and bows, and stranger still to see the assortment of other spirits and their Holiday badges milling around. Charlene realized then that she was looking for someone in particular, and smiled as soon as she spotted the grey fedora.

"Hey!" she said, making her way over to Guy, who looked up with some measure of surprise, clearly and obviously taking in her new outfit. His smile was wide and welcoming as he leaned against a table. He always seemed to be leaning on something, as though he knew he looked good lounging.

"Look at you," he said. "You're figuring things out."

"Shelley helped," Charlene said. "Reminded me—again—that I'm a ghost, not a human. She said it was temporary though. How long does it last?"

Guy pulled the brim of his hat more firmly over his eye.

"I guess we'll find out," he said. "Although I am not quite sure that changing your clothes is the lesson you need to learn."

Charlene focused down on the food spread along the table, an assortment of cakes and snacks that would look at home in any break room, unsure how to respond. How could she still be getting this wrong?

"Want to meet some of the other Holiday Spirits?" Guy asked after a moment. Charlene perked up at that, nodding excitedly.

"I've been so curious to see how the other holidays work," she said, looking around for the tell-tale badges that would let her know which holiday the spirits around her represented.

"Well, these are just the trainees," Guy said, "so I'm afraid you won't get that many answers here. But still." He stood up and ushered her toward a cluster of people in pointy hats, jack-o-lantern badges prominently displayed. "Ladies, this is one of our Christmas Spirit trainees, Charlene. Charlene, this is Ella, Andy, and Myla. They're training to be Halloween witches."

"Double, double, toil and trouble," Ella said. "And all that."

Charlene grinned.

"Sounds super witchy," she said encouragingly.

"Oh, well, it's a direct quote," Andy said. "You're probably not a literature person."

Charlene forced herself to keep her grin going.

"You know, it amazes me just how much literature has been showing up in the afterlife," she said. "I guess I should have paid more attention in English class."

"Have you talked to Walzer?" Myla asked. "He has a great theory—"

"About belief," Charlene finished.

"Which really makes all the literary stuff make more sense," Ella said. "I mean, if you think about it." The other two women nodded, and Charlene suppressed an exasperated sigh.

"Sure does," she said. "So much sense!" She realized she was probably laying it on a bit thick to compensate, which became painfully clear when she got nothing but polite smiles in return. "Well, lovely to meet you. Good luck with the witching!"

She picked a random direction to head in and got several feet away before Guy caught up with her.

"I'm not sure how you're managing to blush," he said. "But it would be charming if it wasn't also a little, well, human."

"I don't understand how I could still be bad at small talk in the afterlife," Charlene complained. "Or need a literature degree."

"You're doing fine," Guy said. "Come on, let's meet some fair-folk."

"Fairies?" Charlene asked.

"In training," Guy corrected. "And don't worry—these aren't the Tolkien sort."

Charlene nodded as though she knew what he meant and wondered if maybe it was too late to catch up on some reading.

CHAPTER NINE
Step into Christmas

Charlene's tour among the other Holiday Spirit trainees left her feeling pretty unsatisfied. It was difficult to ask any meaningful questions with Guy standing next to her. But it was also apparent pretty quickly that the other trainees were at least as lost as she was, if possibly better read. They had all died in holiday-related accidents, though only one person really wanted to talk about it, and Charlene suspected it was because he wanted to reassure himself that death by keg stand was holiday-related enough to count. Considering he was drinking green beer, it apparently was. From what she could gather, none of the other holidays seemed to be quite as particular about what it meant to be a spirit as Christmas was—but they also seemed to have less opportunity to go back down to Earth.

It wasn't long before Charlene was ready to go back to the Hall of Christmas Spirits, where she at least was starting to catch on to some of the rules and where she wasn't forced to make small talk about various types of ceremonial candles. Or try very hard to both avoid flirting with Guy and to not watch him effortlessly flirt with others.

She left Guy behind talking to a group of men who seemed to be training to be the drunken visions most commonly associated with a festival that included lots of drinking and willed herself back among the other Christmas Spirits. She was pleased to see the giant tree pop into view, its mysterious ornaments swirling and floating lights flickering. But when she looked around, she couldn't find a familiar face. She went back to the tree to look—carefully—at the ornaments, leaning in close to try to see the memories inside the swirls. She wasn't sure, but she thought she could just about make out one that seemed to be of a family going sledding.

"You're not one to leave well enough alone, are you?" Guy said from behind her.

"I didn't touch them this time," Charlene said. She stepped back to show that her hands were firmly behind her back. "I was just curious."

"Aren't you always," Guy said, smiling. "Come on, time to see the Future." He reached out a hand. "I think we can skip the hallways and doors, don't you?"

Charlene placed her hand in his and waited for what she was sure would happen next. As she assumed, they were instantly transported to another strange little room. A small group sat in high-backed chairs in a loose circle, each dressed in black and with hoods up around their faces, making it nearly impossible to tell one from another. They each were bent over and working something over in their hands. The room around them seemed strangely dark, and Charlene couldn't get a sense of how high or wide it was. The shadows in the corner seemed deeper and darker than she thought they could be, especially when she couldn't identify any light source making the shadows.

"Hi," Charlene said. Several heads tuned toward her at the

sound of her voice, butmost stayed bent over their work. The ones that turned to look at her seemed to take her in, and then turned back away.

Charlene looked over at Guy, who gestured her forward with his hat, back in his hand. She wondered if taking his hat off was a show of respect, or maybe a way to differentiate himself from the hood-wearing ghosts. She stepped closer and was finally able to see what each of them seemed so intent on working on: they were knitting. What they were knitting was harder to tell, as they all seemed to be using black yarn that blended into their black clothing. She thought she saw trails of something falling off some of the laps, but everything was obscured in darkness.

"Hello?" Charlene ventured again. This time no heads turned toward her.

"Do they talk?" she asked, coming back to Guy and whispering as she got closer to him.

"They can. And they are, in a way, with each other. But they are talking in the future, and it's hard for the rest of us to follow along."

"They are talking about the future?" Charlene asked.

"In the future. It can be very confusing."

He stepped forward, and Charlene noticed that for the very first time, Guy appeared to be nervous.

"We have a new trainee," he said to no one ghost in particular. "And I was hoping one of you might be willing to take her with you on one of your visits."

Charlene couldn't be sure, but she thought that maybe several of them seemed to knit faster, and she wondered if that was one of the ways they communicated with each other. Whatever the discussion was, it ended when one of them stood up. He was tall and thin, and his outfit was an oversized black hoodie over black jeans. Though she was sure he had been holding silver knitting needles before, his hands were now empty, and he used one to point toward one of the dark shadows in the corner of the room.

"There you go," Guy said, coming back to Charlene. "He's gonna take you with him. Just go where he tells you, and probably try not talking."

Charlene stared at the black-clad figure, and then turned back to Guy.

"And this is my last chance to avoid being a Marley?" she asked.

"Very last chance," he said. He twirled the brim of his hat in his hands. "It's not so bad," he told her. "No chains. And eventually, they move on, just like all the other Holiday Spirits."

Charlene looked back over all the black-clad figures in their deep hoods.

"How would you know?" she asked. "They all look alike."

Guy laughed, but it sounded more nervous than amused.

"Go on then, before he changes his mind."

Charlene pulled her jacket tighter around herself, buttoning up the buttons, then shoving her hands deep into her pockets. The hooded man walked toward the shadows, gesturing with one finger for her to follow. She did, and watched as he seemed to disappear into the darkness. She tried to remember all the other things she had done since dying, and that she was already dead and had nothing left to fear, and followed him.

The dark seemed to last a long time, and when Charlene emerged on the other side, she found herself not in another bedroom, but outside in the light grey of early dawn. There was a woman near her and the hooded man, who was around sixty years old and dressed in a long nightgown and slippers. She looked dazed, and had yet to spot the spirits. Charlene turned her head to watch what the ghost was going to do, and was shocked to discover that she suddenly had a black hood of her own. She looked down and saw that the rest of her outfit had changed as well, her tank top, jacket, jeans, and boots now all sooty black. She still had three-quarter sleeves though, and her jacket was more or less the same shape—with the addition of the hood—which would have amused Charlene more if the Ghost of Christmas Future wasn't pointing at the woman.

Charlene opened her mouth to speak, but no sounds came out. She tried again and again, her hand gesturing to her throat to try to make it clear to the other ghost what was happening to her. He pointed at the woman again, his gesture adamant. So Charlene walked toward the woman, unsure of what she was supposed to do next.

The woman seemed to see Charlene then, and turned toward her.

"I am in the presence of the Ghost of Christmas Yet to Come?" she asked. Charlene couldn't say anything in return, so she nodded back. She wondered why the woman could see her, and if she could see the other ghost as well. She got her answer when the other ghost passed between the woman and Charlene, walking in a very specific direction. Not sure what else to do, Charlene pointed after it. The woman looked where her hand was pointing.

"You want me to go there?"

Charlene pointed more emphatically. Yes lady, I want you to go there, she thought.

"Oh, Ghost of the Future," the woman said shakily. "I fear you most of all."

Charlene couldn't blame the woman—hooded and silent was pretty creepy. But the other ghost was moving further away, so she started walking in the same direction, hoping the woman would follow. She did, much closer than Charlene was comfortable with, practically shadowing Charlene as she walked.

Charlene wanted to turn around and tell the woman to back off, but it was as if she didn't have full control over her body. She could move her hand up and down, and she could point, and move her head slightly. But she couldn't speak, or run, or do anything outside of a prescribed set of motions. It was becoming increasingly frustrating, and when the Future Ghost stopped walking and pointed again, clearly indicating where it wanted Charlene to lead the older woman, Charlene stopped and didn't point.

"What is it, Spirit? What do you want me to see?" The woman peered around. Charlene did as well, as much she was able to, but as far as she could tell there really wasn't anything near them. They were in a park of some sort, in the middle of a grass field. There were no people nearby, or anything interesting to look at. The Ghost of Christmas Future pointed again, and again Charlene refused to raise her arm.

"Spirit?" the woman asked questioningly. Charlene felt bad for her. She knew this was supposed to be the grand finale of the whole ordeal that the woman was going through, the thing that was going to fully convince her to change her ways. In fact, if Charlene remembered correctly, the whole thing was supposed to end in some sort of graveyard—the threat of mortality had long been used to get people to behave better—but Charlene couldn't see any gravestones from where she was standing.

"Oh Spirit, what is it you want from me?" the woman asked. She was starting to sound scared, more so than before, and again the Ghost of Christmas Spirit pointed in a direction. There was definitely an air of annoyance to his pointing. Something about that triggered something inside of Charlene, and she raised her hand, and put up a single finger, aimed directly at the other ghost.

"What the hell?" the woman asked. Charlene dropped her hand quickly. She hadn't meant that for the woman. "Well screw you too!" the woman said, and turned and stormed back the way they had come. The Ghost of Christmas Future ran after her, flipping Charlene the bird in return as he passed.

Charlene suddenly felt a tension leave her body, and she looked down to see her clothes returning to their original colors.

"Son of a…" she said, but stopped as soon as she saw Guy approaching her. His hat was on and he didn't look happy.

"I couldn't talk," she said. "Or move, except for like three movements. And the stupid other ghost didn't even tell me he was putting me to work, just kept pointing and wanting me to point in the same direction. And he changed my clothes. And did I mention that I couldn't talk?"

"Charlene Marie Dickenson," Guy said. He pulled a hand-kerchief out of his pocket and wiped his brow, lifting his hat slightly to do so. Charlene was positive she had never seen him sweat before. "If I wasn't already dead, you'd be the death of me."

"I just don't think I'm cut out to be a Ghost of Christmas Future," Charlene said. "I don't even know how to knit."

"You just had to follow," Guy said, stuffing the kerchief back into his pocket and putting his hat back on his head. "That's all. Just follow."

"Look, I have an idea," Charlene said, a rush of fear climbing up her spine. "I have a way out of this."

"There is no way out of this," Guy said. "You knew that going in."

"We go back to Nomura," Charlene said. "And I can tell her just how sorry I am. Thinking about it, really thinking about it, I'm meant to be a Ghost of Christmas Past. I mean, obvious-ly. I'm obsessed with the past. I love the past. People have told me I suck at letting the past go."

"She already said no," Guy said, not unkindly.

"So we ask another ghost. One of them will say yes, and then I'll be a Ghost of Christmas Past. It will work. I promise. We just have to go back and…"

She realized then that they were back in the Hall of Christmas Spirits, back in fact in her little room. One moment out in a field, the other in a room. Things were moving too fast.

"Okay, great, so then we find the other spirits, and…." Charlene nearly tripped, putting out a hand on the bedframe to steady herself. She looked down to see what she had tripped on and saw a short grey chain wrapped around her foot.

"No," she said. "No. I have a plan, a chance. No!" She tried to shake the chain off, but it clung on. And then it grew. It slithered up her leg, like a snake, the links getting thicker and heavier as it went. Each part of her the chain links touched seemed to tarnish into metallic grey, and she watched in horror as all the color left her pants, her shirt, and then the very skin of her arm. "No," she said again, a hoarse whisper of denial. But the chain kept growing, winding itself around her waist, draping off her shoulders, and falling back to the floor like an anchor.

Charlene looked up at Guy, the horror in her eyes mirrored by the sorrow in his.

"I'm so sorry," he said. "I truly am."

CHAPTER TEN
Blue Christmas

The knock on Charlene's door was gentle, and hesitant, and it was easy to guess who the person on the other side of her door was. Charlene had no interest in talking to Shelley, though part of her knew she should. There were lessons to be learned about being a Marley, lessons like how to carry the chain, how to keep yourself from constantly tripping over it, how not to scream into eternity about the unfairness of it all. The hesitant knock sounded again, and then once more. And then, as Charlene hoped, there was a faint sound of a heavy weight being dragged away.

Marleys didn't sleep. That was something that Charlene had figured out early on. No matter how long she stared up at her ceiling—and she assumed she'd been staring up for quite some time—her eyelids never got heavy, and dreamland never beckoned. She wasn't sure this was unique to Marleys. It was a fair assumption that ghosts in general didn't sleep, but she attributed it to being a Marley, because right now she attributed all her misery to being a Marley.

After a while, a much more confident and declarative knock came through her door. Guy, Charlene guessed. This was confirmed when she heard him call to her. She didn't answer, and had no intention of answering, and though he knocked a few more times and called her name again, he respected her closed door and didn't manifest in her room as she assumed he could. And then, she assumed, he went away.

It was difficult to find a good position to lie in as a Marley. There seemed to be some unspoken rule about how much surface of her body Charlene had to have covered in chains. She couldn't take the chain off, and only ever seemed to be able to unwind a certain amount of it before her efforts to continue to unwind seemed to have the paradoxical effect of putting the chain back on her. As such, she had to use an assortment of pillows to prop herself up in a way that was almost comfortable, or about as comfortable as she was going to be able to achieve in her current state. But once propped just so, she found that she could stare up at the ceiling almost indefinitely, letting her thoughts wander up and down the path of choices that lead her to her singularly miserable current state.

The easiest and shortest path she wished she could change was not following Stephen on the day that she died. A slightly longer path had her getting over him sooner, and an even longer path had her never dating him in the first place. She tried to think of other variables that also could have helped her avoid an untimely death, including having an even better therapist, going out on more dates before, after, and in some fantasy versions in her head, while dating Stephen. Sometimes she imagined what moving to a different city might have done for the course of her life. Other times she played out some sort of butterfly effect—making one small change and seeing if that could make a difference, such as changing which coffee shop she stopped at on the day she died.

Now and then, Charlene was able to think about the choices she made since dying, but since these were the most recent—and the rawest—it was harder for her to face them. She found it difficult to imagine never trying to see her sister, or not feeling awkward standing in the middle of a church, regardless if people could see her or not. Try as she might though, she could never actually regret her actions as a trainee Ghost of Christmas Future, and in her most generous moments realized that living as a shadow might actually be a worse fate than living—or after-living—with chains.

Charlene moved her hip slightly, easing it over a pernicious steel boot that had wedged itself behind her. All those times when she was so excited to be feeling again mocked her now. Marleys had full use of all their senses, and all of them informed her of the weight, and metallic smell, of her chain. She had more or less guessed correctly about what sorts of items would end up on her chain. As Shelley had warned, these items weren't what gave her the chain, they were just the things most easily cast in steel. Sometimes, the only thing that Charlene imagined changing was her Earthly interests so that she might have better shaped items on her chain.

She really ought to have read more, she thought. Books were so nice and flat. Done right, she could even have made a bed of them.

A knock knock knock on Charlene's door made her turn her head. It wasn't Shelley or Guy, and she couldn't imagine who else might want to visit her. Then she heard the knock again, and a third time, before finally catching on to the pattern—the knock always came in threes.

"Walzer?" she called out.

Three voices responded in the affirmative.

"Yes."

Charlene couldn't imagine what Walzer could possibly want, and because she couldn't imagine it, she went through the arduous tasks of sitting up, a noisy and painful action.

"Come in," she called out, once she had her chain mostly settled.

Walzer looked the same as the last time she saw him, though somehow the three-in-one movements bothered her less than before. His younger self gave a little wave, his oldest a small bow of his head, but the middle Walzer just stood awkwardly inside her door.

"You can sit, if you want," Charlene said, gesturing toward the chair by the desk, and wincing as a steel bobble-head doll of one of her favorite characters slipped free and wrenched her arm down. She brought it back in toward her body clumsily, cradling it against her stomach. "I'd get up, but…"

"You're still adjusting," Walzer finished. He made his way to the chair, politely stepping over a coil of chain on the floor, and two-thirds of him managed not to stare. The youngest set of his eyes seemed alarmed though.

"I'm surprised to see you," Charlene said.

"I'm a bit surprised myself," he countered, two sets of his legs crossing themselves, and the third sprawling wide, until one of the older hands slapped his youngest knee, causing that version of himself to fall in line. "I really thought that things would go differently for you."

"Did you?" Charlene asked. "I'm the girl who ran through the presentation. I kind of think the warning signs were there that following the rules was going to be difficult for me."

Two of his heads nodded, and the third grinned.

"Still, I can't help but feeling I have some fault in this," he said. "I should have prepared you better, really helped you understand the stakes."

"Shelley warned me the best she could," Charlene said. "She even let me hold part of her chain once, get the heft of it."

"That was generous of her," Walzer said. "Marleys are usually so private about their chains. For good reason of course." Two of his faces made a point of not looking to closely at the items bound up in Charlene's chain, though she was surprised that it was the oldest set of eyes that was having the hardest time with his curiosity.

"You can look, I don't mind." She held up a length of chain that had overgrown ticket stubs to one of her favorite movies dangling off it. "It's like the world's heaviest scrap book. Sort of seems like it was meant to be shared."

Walzer leaned forward, peering at different items.

"I've talked with several Marleys, as you know," he said. "And I have a theory about the chains. If you want to hear it."

"Sure," Charlene said.

"The items on the chain aren't important because of what they are—like those ticket stubs. They are important because of what they represent. If you don't mind my asking, why was that movie in particular so important to you?"

Charlene twisted the steel around to read the engraving on it, as though she didn't already know which movie name would be posted on there.

"It was my first date with Stephen," she said. "First official date. We'd met at a party, at a friend's house. There was drinking, and some drunken making out, and I thought that was going to be it. But he sought me out, messaged me, asked me out. And we went to this movie."

"And this Stephen was important to you?"

"Very," she said, running her fingers over the edges of the words, feeling them out.

"I apologize now for this next question, but it helps with my theory. Were you and Stephen perhaps not together at the time of your death?"

Charlene looked up at Walzer, her brows crinkled together.

"We'd been broken up for some time," she said. "It was a rough break up. I'd had a hard time…" She let her voice drift off.

"Letting go," Walzer finished for her. "Yes, I thought as much. From what I can tell, almost all the items on the chains represent something that in life the Marley struggled with letting go of. I know one Marley who has an inordinate amount of school papers with poor grades attached to him."

"Oh?" Charlene said. She hoped he couldn't see her own version of that—an exceptionally scathing performance review from a certain prior supervisor—attached to a chain link behind her. "I guess it's too late to let those things go, now," she added, shifting her weight a little to continue to hide the performance review.

"I suppose," Walzer said, but all of his faces looked thoughtful.

"I mean, no one has ever stopped being a Marley," Charlene said, watching his faces. "Or shortened their chain."

Walzer's faces continued to demonstrate that he was thinking very hard.

"Walzer?" she asked quietly, not wanting to disturb his thought process.

"Well, I do wonder," he said. "You know my theory about why this place exists."

"Belief," Charlene said. "A theory I think there is a lot of support for." She remembered how she was able to fly because she believed she could, how she walked through doors because she assumed that's what ghosts could do.

"Well, I just wonder if maybe belief is also what's making the chains." He poked at one with the toe of three of his feet, causing it to move three times. "If you believe you can't let these things go, then of course you can't. But maybe if you believed...differently." He poked again, and again the chain moved three times, rattling up to Charlene and making her grind her teeth at the sensation.

"Don't do that," she said, more sternly than she meant to. All three faces looked very apologetic and Walzer moved his feet carefully under his chair.

"I'm not sure how one believes in their ability to let things go," Charlene said after her chain settled.

"Oh, I think it's simpler than that," Walzer said. "I think you just—let things go."

Right. Sure. Simple.

Charlene tried not to slump in defeat, but mostly because then parts of her chain that she'd just gotten settled would poke into her if she did.

"That is a good theory," Charlene said. "I don't suppose you've shared it with other people? Who maybe, successfully, tested it?"

Walzer shook his heads.

"I have shared it, yes, but so far no one has really managed to get rid of their chains."

Charlene sighed.

"Still, the whole point is—maybe there's hope." Walzer gave Charlene an encouraging smile. She smiled back, because that was what people did when others were being kind.

"Well, I appreciate you taking the time to come and see me, and tell me about your theory," she said. Her words had the desired effect and Walzer stood up, nodding with understanding.

"Of course," he said, making his way over to the door and avoiding her chain as he went. "Anything I can do to help." He paused before leaving. "Really, Charlene. Anything. I really wish…."

But he didn't have to say what he really wished. They both really wished it. Charlene managed a more genuine smile.

"I really do appreciate it," she said. She watched as each

Walzer face softened with kindness and sympathy, and then watched the Trip turn and leave.

Charlene contemplated lying down again, but decided it would be too much work. So instead she stared at the blank shelves above her little desk and contemplated Walzer's theory. What would it take to let go?

But she had spent years in therapy asking that same question and never finding any specific solution. "Just let it go" sounded super easy, but in practice was super hard. How did she stop thinking about things when the thoughts came unbidden into her head? How did she get over feelings, when they landed sharp and sudden in her chest, at the most inopportune times? How did she just stop feeling hurt, or ashamed, or guilty?

Time was supposed to play a part in all this, as therapists and friends alike told her over and over again to just give herself time.

But then the time had run out. And now, in a way, she had all of time ahead of her, and yet no more idea how to use that time to shed even a single link on her chain.

What she really wanted to do, what she felt was the actual answer to everything, was to forget. It would be easy to let go of things if she couldn't actually remember them. She wondered if there was such a thing as a ghost lobotomy.

Charlene looked around her little room, the same walls she had been staring at for who knows how long, ever since her chain appeared. Whatever answer there was to this mess, she wasn't going to find it here. So she gathered up her chain, looping it around her arms and shoulders, and stood up.

Standing wasn't easy, as she felt unbalanced and overly cumbersome, but after a moment, the weight of what she carried settled more easily around her. It was heavy, sure, but somehow her ghost self was strong enough to carry it. Slowly but surely she walked to the door. There, she hesitated.

She had gotten used to just walking through doors, but was no longer sure that was possible. She'd never seen Shelley walk through a closed door. Maybe the chains couldn't go through.

On the other hand, trying to find a way to shift her chain and get a hand free to turn the knob seemed like an awful lot of work. Charlene contemplated her options. If she walked forward and the chain got stuck, she'd just walk backward again and then go for the knob. And if she walked forward and banged into the door, it wasn't like it was going to kill her.

Charlene walked forward. She had that familiar sense of darkness as she walked through solid wood, and then she was on the other side. She kept walking, turning slightly to watch as the last of her chain slowly scraped along the floor, fully clearing the door.

Well, that was something at least. She may be a Marley, she thought, but she was still a ghost.

She headed off to find Shelley and compare notes. It was time to embrace her fate—and maybe find a way to change it.

CHAPTER ELEVEN
Christmas Time is Here

Charlene wandered into the Hall of Christmas Spirits, searching the various clusters of people standing around the center tree for familiar faces. She spotted two Trips—a rare sight for her—but neither was Walzer. There were a handful of Marleys, but it took her a while to find Shelley. She was standing with another Marley, who Charlene recognized from her training session with Nomura. Shelley waved as soon as she saw Charlene, a belabored movement thanks to her chain.

"So good to see you out and about, honey!" Shelley called. "I know how hard the first little while is."

"I didn't leave my room for so long, they held an intervention," the other Marley said. Their hair was longer in the front than the back and hung into their eyes a little but it softened the angles of their face. Charlene was surprised by how young they looked—maybe as old as early 20s, maybe even younger that. It made her sad to think of someone dying so young. They gave Charlene a warm smile. They were wearing jeans, a t-shirt, and Doc Martens—all greyed out thanks to being a Marley—and Charlene couldn't get a sense of what time period they might be from. "I'm Jeri, by the way," they said. "We were never properly introduced before."

Charlene nodded her head in acknowledgement, which

seemed like it would take the least amount of effort, and hoped she wasn't coming off as rude. Jeri smiled back, so she figured they understood Charlene's reluctance to move.

"How did that turn out anyway? With your cousin?"

"Oh the usual—the visits almost always work, at least for a little while."

Charlene frowned.

"Only a little while?" she asked. Jeri gave Shelley a questioning look, and Shelley shrugged back.

"Better she knows," she said.

"Knows what?" Charlene asked.

"I don't want you to think that the visits don't help people, because they do," Jeri said. "We give people a chance to see things they wouldn't otherwise see. They get to revisit their pasts, take stock of their presents, and get totally freaked out by their futures. And they wake up refreshed and motivated to change."

"And for a while, they do," Shelley said.

"But change is hard. It takes consistent effort to maintain, because of how powerful all the old ways of being and thinking are. They can pull people back, you know?" Jeri shook their head. "I'm not saying one night can't change someone's entire life. It can. But they kinda have to participate in that change too. And for some folks—well, it's just harder for some folks than others."

Charlene wished she could say she was surprised. It actually all made perfect sense.

"But what we do matters though, right? I'd hate to think

I'll be in chains for all eternity and not actually make a difference."

"Oh, it definitely matters," Jeri said. "And at least when you're a Marley, you get to go back and see people you knew. I mean, just to warn them, but still. It's nice to catch up a little."

"Do Marleys ever visit people they didn't know in life?"

"That would ruin the point," Shelley said. "It's a warning from someone who knew them."

"So what happens when all the people you know are gone?"

Shelley and Jeri looked at each other, as if trying to decide which one was going to tell Charlene.

"Oh," she said. "Then there's no one to visit."

"No more Earth trips," Jeri said. "But you can still talk to the other ghosts. It's not like you'll be alone."

"But I won't have purpose anymore," Charlene said. Her chains seemed to feel extraordinarily heavy just then. "For the rest of eternity."

Jeri shifted their chains and stepped forward, putting their hand on Charlene's shoulder.

"It's going to be okay," Jeri said. "You'll see."

"How?" Charlene asked. Jeri shrugged.

"I just believe it will be," they said. After a moment, they moved their hand back, readjusting their chains. Charlene couldn't help but notice the steel music sheets and instruments, including a rather cumbersome miniature piano. Chains gave you one advantage at least, she thought. They helped you know something about the person wearing them.

"Anyway, it's not so bad, honey," Shelley said. "You have us!" She grinned at Charlene, and it was such a goofy grin that it surprised a giggle from Charlene.

"So," she said to the others. "What do Marleys do around here for fun?"

"Rattle our chains and moan, mostly," Jeri said. Charlene laughed again.

"They aren't kidding," Shelley said. "It really annoys the other spirits, especially the Ghosts of Christmas Future."

"Man, I hate those guys," Charlene said.

"Walzer keeps trying to tell me they aren't so bad, but I'm not convinced," Jeri said.

Charlene nodded agreement.

"And I supposed at some point another Holiday Spirit will come here, and maybe I can be the Marley for them, the way Shelley was for me," she said, thinking through the possibilities of her afterlife.

"Yeah honey! That's the spirit!" Shelley said. Jeri groaned at the pun.

"And I suppose I could get in on whatever bets you and Guy have going next time," Charlene added, remembering back to her trip to her own personal Christmas past.

"Oh, yeah," Shelley said. But her voice was very different than it was before, and Charlene could have sworn she seemed suddenly uncomfortable. Jeri was giving her a very peculiar look.

And then something clicked.

"Ten what?" Charlene asked.

"What honey?" Shelley responded, gathering her chains and clearly looking like she was trying to leave. "You know I got things I gotta get to. Totally slipped my mind."

"Ten what?" Charlene asked again, putting herself directly in front of Shelley and arranging her chains to ty to give her more mass, become a large barrier. "You bet Guy a ten-er that I wouldn't run. But I did, and then you said, 'that's ten I'll never get back.' Ten of what?"

She knew the answer wasn't money—Christmas Spirits didn't need things like that. Just like they didn't need food or sleep or anything that mortals spent so much of their time and energy on.

"Just forget about it," Jeri said, shaking their head. "You're not ready for the Memory Machine."

Charlene glared at Jeri.

"Ready or not, I want to know. What the hell is a Memory Machine?" She wasn't sure why she was feeling so strongly about this, but she was. Maybe it was left over anger and shame about becoming a Marley. Maybe it was more of the defiance that helped her get her chains in the first place. But if Charlene didn't think putting her hands on her hips would cause a cascade of chains, she would have done so just for the effect. "Ten. Of. What?"

Jeri stared hard at Shelley, clearly telling her with all their being not to say anything. But Shelley just sighed, and Charlene knew she'd won.

"Best if I just show you," she said. "Or rather, show you *why* I can't show you."

"Oh hell no," Jeri said. "I won't have any part of this. You know she's not ready." Jeri gathered up their chain, throwing what looked like a steel ukulele over their shoulder, and started to shamble away. "It's a very bad idea!" they said over their shoulder.

"Jeri is right about that," Shelley said.

"It's amazing how knowing something is a bad idea has never stopped me before," Charlene said. "And like Jeri said, change is hard. So I guess I'm just gonna keep up with my bad ideas." She looked at Shelley expectantly. The other ghost looked utterly defeated.

"Fine," she said. "But you really ought to rethink that whole bad idea thing."

Charlene agreed, but wasn't going to tell Shelley that. Instead she followed the specter around the Christmas tree and toward the white pearlescent door that Guy had so clearly led her away from on her first trip to the hall.

"The answer to 'ten of what' is behind that door, along with what is a Memory Machine," Shelley said. "But you won't be able to get through it anyway. No door handle, and no way to open it." She seemed pleased with this information.

Charlene gave her a wry look.

"I'm a ghost. I don't need door handles." And before Shelley could stop her, she walked forward, hoping this door would be as easy to pass through as the one to her little bedroom. Confidence was key, she decided, so she didn't hesitate as the white material got closer and closer, and only closed her eyes briefly right before she would either make contact or pass through. To her great relief, nothing slammed into her, and she opened her eyes in time to take in an encompassing white light before emerging into an open space. She dutifully turned to pull the rest of her chain through the door as well, coiling it around her arm to keep it from dragging too much behind her before facing the rest of the room.

It was an odd shape, roughly oval with rounded walls that curved up to a high ceiling. In the center was a strange device in the same white material as the door, with strange mechanical arms and exposed gold gears. Most of it was moving, taking colored blobs from what looked like a pneumatic tube coming down from the ceiling and putting them on some sort of conveyor belt where another arm seemed to magically encase them in glass. At this point, Charlene recognized the ornaments from the tree in the hall. This apparently was the device that made them, and the weird globs then somehow were globs of memories. This, then, was the Memory Machine.

Charlene turned, expecting Shelley to come into the room with her, but there was still no sign of her. So Charlene moved closer to the machine to get a better look and better idea of how it could possibly be working. While most of it was dedicated to moving and encasing the memory blobs coming down the tube, another part of it had something to do with a wide bench in the middle and a series of arms that could possibly be used to move…something…to the person in the middle.

"You're not ready for this," Guy said behind her. Charlene had long gotten used to his sudden appearances and didn't flinch at the sound of his voice. He was wearing his hat and suit jacket, and looked very serious.

"So I've been told," she said, facing him. "But what is it? And what does it have to do with the bet you made with Shelley?"

"It's the Memory Machine," he said, confirming Charlene's guess. He took a long moment to look at the various arms, and walked closer to them, running his hand over one of the stationary ones. "Mostly, it moves the memories that get collected—and no, I don't know how—and turns them into ornaments. As you can see."

"And this part here?" Charlene asked, pointing out the chair in the middle. "It this related to what Shelley bet you?"

"Yes," Guy said, though he didn't sound sure. "The Memory Machine allows ghosts to experience some of those memories."

"Other people's memories?" Charlene asked.

"Eternity is a long time," Guy said. "A lot of the spirits, especially the Marleys who have been around for a while, get bored. More than bored. Desperate for something, some break from the same thing over and over again. So they come here, and for a moment, live someone else's memory."

Charlene felt there must be something ethically wrong with this—a violation of privacy at the very least—but at the same time, she understood how boredom could drive someone to it.

"Whose memories?"

"People's," Guy said. "Who are no longer living. Their memories—well, their Christmas memories—get stored on the tree."

"There's not enough ornaments on the tree for all those memories," Charlene said, watching as the conveyor belt constantly moved along, a steady stream of memory blobs passing by them.

"Of course not," Guy said. "Most of them just get stored. The ones on the tree rotate. We're not sure how, we just know that they do. Something also color codes them—silver, gold, red, green, blue, and purple, like you've seen. That part appears to be random."

"And so you sit here, and then what?"

"You're not ready to see other people's memories," he said gently.

"Why not?" Charlene wasn't angry, just curious.

"You are still too wrapped up in your own."

Charlene probably agreed with that. She imagined that whatever the machine did, it wouldn't be like watching a movie or TV show. She also imagined that seeing other people's memories—happy or sad—would just make her miss her own family even more than she already did. It didn't help that the bench and arms looked more than a little intimidating, and she still couldn't imagine how they could possibly work.

But that's not why she was asking about the machine.

"Can the machine take our memories?" she asked.

"That's not what it's designed to do," Guy responded, which Charlene noticed didn't actually mean no.

"And you bet Shelley ten memories?"

"She bet me," he said, clarifying. "There's a limit to how

many you are allowed to see per season. She just gave up ten of hers."

"So you got them—ten memories that belong to someone else." Charlene didn't like how any of this sounded. "And you're just going to take them from Shelley. Just like this machine took them from…someone else."

"Look, you need time. More Christmas seasons. Then you can come back here, try the Memory Machine out. But right now, you're still adjusting to being here, and being a Marley."

"All I need is time," Charlene said. She'd heard that before. So many times before. "One last question, and then we can leave."

"Can we then?" Guy said with a wry laugh.

"How come you came in, and not Shelley? Couldn't she have told me all the same things?"

Guy shifted his weight, a sign Charlene took to mean he was uncomfortable with the question.

"I thought you'd hear it better from me," he said.

"But what are you? Who are you? You're not a Ghost of Christmas Past, Present, or Future. You're not a Marley. You're not a Trip."

"I'm a trainer."

"Are you the only one? How do you even get to be a trainer?"

Guy adjusted his hat, looking away from Charlene in the process.

"You said one last question and then we'd leave."

Charlene stared at him for a long moment and eventually

he met her gaze. It seemed like they were engaged in a battle of wills, but Charlene wondered if she was the only one feeling that. She looked away first.

"I did say that," she said. She headed toward the white door and didn't even pause before walking through it.

Shelley was waiting nervously on the other side, and only seemed to relax when she saw Guy emerge from behind Charlene.

"Get what you needed, honey?" she asked Charlene.

"Yeah," Charlene said. "I believe I did."

CHAPTER TWELVE
All I Want for Christmas is You

There was no real sense of day or night in the Hall of Christmas Spirits, but there did seem to be a general order to things. Time could be measured by the changing of the ornaments on the Christmas tree, or by the fashion changes of the Ghosts of Christmas Present. It was always "the holiday season" in the Hall of Christmas Spirits, but obviously it couldn't always be back down on Earth. There was a busy time, when ghosts went out constantly on assignment, and a slow time, when people went to the Memory Machine, or stood around chatting. All of this was painful for Charlene. Her chain was quite literally a drag, slowing down her movements and pressing down on flesh that was feeling all too much. It made her long for those early moments when she couldn't feel her body, which is something she never thought she'd miss. Shelley insisted that she would adjust to the weight of her chain "in time", but Charlene was getting tired of waiting for time to do whatever magic people assumed it could do.

Instead, she kept watching the room with the Memory Machine. No one ever seemed to go in or out of it without Guy present.

She'd asked Shelley about him, and Jeri, and both had made vague comments. He was really nice. So helpful. They were all so lucky to have such a good trainer.

"Are there any other trainers?" she had asked.

"Why would there be?" Shelley had responded.

"We've only ever needed the one," Jeri had said.

Frustrated by their responses, Charlene sought Walzer out. She found him in his office, editing the welcoming presentation.

"What was it exactly that made it so hard to watch?" he asked her.

"Well, it was slow," she said. "And the letters were giant. And only a few came by at a time, making it hard to put the sentences together."

"Hmmm." He was looking at a large display of the Welcome Message, which took up the entire back wall of his office. Except for the back wall, the rest of the office was still grey, and still didn't have any windows, and still was somewhat depressing to look at. It was also one of the only places in all the Hall that didn't seem covered in Christmas decorations.

"Also, I really didn't like not seeing my body," Charlene said after a moment. "It felt super weird."

"Well, that can't be helped," Walzer said. "It's supposed to help people start to get used to thinking of themselves as ghosts. Bodies just get in the way of that."

His youngest face seemed bored, but the other two were very focused on his task. He did something on his desk that shrunk down the size of the letters on the word WELCOME.

"Better?" he asked.

"It got bigger as it scrolled toward me. I'm not sure how changing the size will help."

Charlene was sprawled out on the low couch against the wall, fiddling with a steel purse attached to her chain.

"What if it scrolled up instead of toward you?" he asked, making more adjustments.

"Probably better," Charlene said. "Though if you gave people a chance to forward through it, like a slideshow…."

"Control the pace of the scrolling? Hmmmm."

Charlotte picked at the steel, wishing that any of the items on her chain could be smaller, or more entertaining to play with.

"No one else has ever run through it?" she asked.

"Not to my knowledge," Walzer replied. "So it could be that no one else ever would. Still, no reason not to try to improve it anyway."

"And did everyone who became a Marley become one for the same reasons?"

"They all struggled to be Ghosts of Christmas Past, Present, or Future. But not for the same reasons, or the same way." Walzer turned away from his desk and leaned back against it, facing Charlene. "Is this just general curiosity, or something else?"

"I'm just trying to make sense of this world," Charlene said. "I feel like there is still so much I don't get."

"Such as?"

"Guy, for one."

All three of Walzer's faces broke out into grins.

"You're not the first to be…curious…about him," he said, his voices rich with amusement. His youngest self seemed to be suppressing a giggle.

"It's not like that!" Charlene protested, glad for her grey coating for once so that he couldn't see her blush. "He's just kind of an anomaly here."

"In what way?" Walzer asked, two sets of him crossing his arms, and the third still trying not to giggle.

"He's the only trainer, for one," Charlene said. "And he appears and disappears wherever he wants, both in the Hall and back on Earth. I get the impression he was never one of the Visiting Ghosts, and obviously he's not a Marley or a Trip—er, Triumvir. He seems to be wholly unique."

"And pretty good looking," Walzer said. "I have noticed you noticing that."

"That's beside the point," Charlene said, pushing a link of chain—along with the steel purse—off her lap. It landed with a thud on the floor in front of her. "I'm pretty sure he once was alive. He said something about 'his New York.' I kinda think maybe he was from there, maybe during the Harlem Renaissance, based on how he's dressed and him saying he preferred Harlem."

"Sure, everyone knows that," Walzer said. "Honestly, I think he may be lying about the no relation thing. He always winks when he says it."

"No relation?"

"To Faulkner? His last name?" Two of Walzer's faces looked disappointed. "I keep forgetting that you're not into literature."

Charlene let the comment go.

"So he's a proper ghost, like you and me. Only, he doesn't

fit any of the other categories here. Is he from another Holiday Hall? How did he get here?"

Walzer shook his head. "He was here when I got here."

Charlene hesitated.

"1998," Walzer said. "Since you were thinking it. And no, I don't want to talk about how I died. None of that really matters anymore, does it?" His oldest self and youngest self looked sad, but his middle self just looked annoyed.

"Okay, then the room with the Memory Machine. How come no one ever goes in there without Guy?"

"Oh, that's easy," Walzer said. "No one else can. He's the only one that the door will open for."

"Yeah, but that doesn't matter, you can just..." Something in Walzer's youngest face made Charlene stop. She wondered, not for the first time, if the three Walzers actually communicated with each other, if it was possible for one of them to know something the others didn't.

"You can just what?" Walzer asked. Well, most of him did.

"Ask him to open the door for you. He doesn't have to go in with you, does he?"

It was a lame recovery attempt, but two-thirds of Walzer seemed satisfied with the response, while the last third seemed relieved.

"I'm pretty sure the machine won't work for anyone but him, either," Walzer said. "I don't know why anyone would try."

"He said I'm not ready to use the machine yet," Charlene said.

"You're not."

"Why not?"

"Well, for one thing, it takes longer for Marleys to be ready, in general. And for another…" It was Walzer's turn to hesitate. "You have been remarkably attached to life," he said. "From your first moment here. You heard sooner, felt sooner. Messed up sooner."

"What do you mean?"

"Most trainees go on several shadowing missions with each ghost type. Ample opportunity to mess up, or to figure out that one type of ghost isn't for you—or you for it. But you—first time out, each time." One set of hands made a motion like he was dropping a ball, another like he was fumbling something, and the youngest drew a finger across his neck, which Charlene thought was a little extreme. "It would be impressive if it wasn't also, well, sad."

"I thought feeling so soon meant I was advanced," Charlene said.

"It meant that you were very, very attached to living. And all that came with it. And well—maybe you were always going to end up a Marley, after all."

Charlene contemplated this.

"And so I'm not ready to experience other people's memories, because I'm still too caught up in my own."

"Exactly," Walzer said. "But if you just…."

"Give it time," Charlene said with him. "Yeah, I know."

She stood up, a tricky affair she had become better at since she got her first chain link, and arranged her chain in such a way that would make it easier to walk.

"Thanks for the talk, as always," she said with a smile. "I'll leave you to your editing."

"Always good to chat with you," Walzer said, and she felt as if all three Walzers genuinely meant it.

Shuffling from his office was a slow methodical affair, but it gave Charlene time to think. Somehow, no one else had ever tried—or succeeded—in getting through the door to the Memory Machine room but her. When she got to the Hall of Christmas Spirits, she very deliberately walked to the side away from the white pearlescent door. She couldn't see it—the tree was very much in the way—but she didn't need to for what she was hoping to do.

Every time she had run as a ghost, she had never run into anything. She simply passed through all objects in her path. And she had moved so fast, she was sure no one would have been able to see her, not with mortal eyes, and she hoped, not with specter eyes either.

Charlene waited until the ghosts closest to her moved away. All the ghosts tended to wander from space to space, particularly the Marleys who found standing still somewhat painful. Once the area around her was mostly clear, Charlene closed her eyes and concentrated, picturing herself zooming through the tree, through the white door, and into the room with the Memory Machine. She pictured the Memory Machine as clearly as she could remember it, focusing on every angle and bend, and pushed herself forward with her mind, toward that room.

She had the slight sensation of movement, and a faint jingling of her chain, and opened her eyes, prepared to be disappointed. Instead, she was staring directly at the Memory Machine in front of her.

Grinning, she did a little dance, merrily shaking her chain before remembering to look behind her and see if all of it had come through the door with her. She cursed as she saw the tail end of it obscured by the white door and yanked her chain hard toward herself. The very end had a steel to-go coffee cup on it, and the cup flew in and bonked Charlene on the head. It hurt. She hated that it hurt, and that she had to move her chains around to rub at the spot on her forehead.

Charlene turned to examine the machine more closely, hoping that she could get what she wanted to get done before Guy found out and did one of his random appearing acts.

The Memory Machine was not an intuitive piece of machinery, and while the conveyor belt function seemed pretty simple, the part with the chair and the presumable ability to put other people's memories in a ghost's head looked complex.

Charlene had no intention of seeing other memories anyway—her goal was to get rid of her own, and her hopefully her chain with it. She would literally let go—by forgetting.

Once her exploration of the chair contraption revealed nothing useful, she turned to the pneumatic tube. Memory globs floated through it on pockets of air before being plucked out by one of the arms and dropped onto the conveyor belt with a soft squish.

Charlene looked up, tracking the tube up into the ceiling. The globs had to come from somewhere. But wandering around the Hall of Christmas Spirits didn't seem like the best way to find out where. Instead, Charlene looked down at her feet and at her chain. It was heavy. She felt it against her skin, a constant pressure, always poking and rubbing.

Where she didn't feel it was in her legs. She never felt tired from wearing it, or sore. If it had been a real chain, back on Earth, she never would have been able to carry it all, but her ghost form did just fine. And all of her, chain included, passed through doors.

So why not ceilings?

Charlene jumped. She landed softly back down on her feet. She jumped again, and while she was sure she had made it higher than before, again she came down. She grabbed hold of one of the stationary arms of the Memory Machine, and this time when she jumped also pulled, as though trying to launch herself into the air. She sprung upward, willing herself higher and higher, until she passed through something solid and gray and emerged through the ceiling of her room and the floor of the room above.

Landing was trickier, as she had to first assure her ghost senses that the floor was solid again, which meant she had to pull her chain all the way through and up off the ground. Finally, she was fully in the room above the one she'd just been in, hovering slightly above the floor.

In this room, a mechanical arm plucked memory blobs from a conveyor belt and dropped them into a pneumatic tube, and this time Charlene followed the belt as it seemed to pass into another room. Going through the wall was much easier than going through the ceiling, and Charlene even managed to land on the floor on the other side, feeling it solid beneath her.

But this room did not have a Memory Machine. Instead it had more of those white and gold mechanical arms, pulling small globs of white pearlescent substances from a glowing white pool in the floor. Each cookie-dough-like blob was then dumped into a another pool of gold, silver, red, green, blue or purple before being plucked out again and put on the conveyor belt.

Charlene stared at the pool. What she needed was whatever thing put the memories into the pool. She stepped forward to get a closer look, feeling more comfortable with the pace of walking than floating, and tripped over the edge of her own chain. She stumbled forward and caught herself on a mechanical arm, which seemed indifferent to her weight and continued on its journey anyway. But while she managed to stop her body from falling into the pool, she couldn't stop a loop of chain from falling in.

She heard a hissing sound, and saw a small tendril of smoke drift up from where the chain hit the mysterious white liquid. Charlene pulled back the end of her chain and saw with horrified fasciation what looked like a melted end. There was still white liquid on the end of it, and instead of dripping off, it seemed to drip on, pouring itself up the steel link. It ate the metal as it went, leaving a trail of smoke behind.

Charlene stepped back from the pool and dropped the chain end, suddenly scared. She watched with terror as the white liquid continued to consume her chain, link by link, steel item by steel item. She pulled as much of her chain from her as she could, trying to figure out how long she had until the liquid reached her. She had four feet of chain left. Then three. Then two. She tried to pull more of the chain off, but that same glue that meant she could never really remove it kept it firmly in place, and the white liquid was getting closer and closer to what she still thought of as her skin.

"Help!" she called out. "Guy! Help!"

He appeared almost instantly, hat in hand, a concerned look on his face. And then he saw Charlene's chain and the white liquid. He shoved his hat on his head and reached out, wrenching Charlene's chain from her body. The liquid kept climbing, and white smoke circled all around them as Guy pulled link after link from Charlene's skin. She could feel it ripping away like it was clumps of hair, and she couldn't help crying out in both pain and fear.

"Almost!" Guy said, and Charlene couldn't tell if that meant he was almost done freeing her from her chain or that the liquid was almost to her body. She closed her eyes against the smoke, the pain, and her fear, and screamed.

"There!" Guy said, yanking her away from the pool and cradling her body close to his, her head pressed against his chest. He was smoothing down her hair with his hands, murmuring soft words. "It's okay, you're okay. It's over now, you're okay."

Charlene watched as the white liquid consumed the last of her chain. Then, seemingly satisfied, it began to slowly trickle back toward the pool, every last drop of it returning from where it came.

"I'm sorry," Charlene said. "I'm so sorry!" She was sobbing, felt hot tears roll down her cheeks. "I didn't know. I was just looking. I didn't know."

She looked up at Guy, managing to stay in the circle of his arms as she did so. He wiped tears from her cheek, and the shock of the intimacy of this touch quieted her tears and slowed the deep breaths she just realized she had been taking. And for one amazing moment she realized—she'd done it. She'd gotten rid of her chain! And now she was in Guy's arms, and he was looking at her not with anger but with....

Sadness. Profound, pitying, sadness.

Charlene pushed against him, breaking his hold. He stepped back to give her space.

"I'm very sorry," he said.

Charlene shook her head. She looked down at her body, now free from the chain and somehow in the process back to normal colors—the green of her tank top, the cream of her jacket, the blue of her jeans, the outfit that should have been temporary but that never changed back—and then back up at Guy. Why was he so sad? Why was he so sorry?

"I don't understand," she said. And at the same time: "I don't get it" and "What's happening?"

Charlene's hand flew to her mouth. And then it flew to her mouth. And then it flew to her mouth. She put the other one out in front of her, and watched her hand do the same motion twice more. Only then did she notice the small differences: one hand had nail polish, a different color on every finger, making a rainbow. One was clear of nail, and normal of flesh. But the third seemed to have thinner skin that looked both wrinkled and puffy at the same time.

"What the heck/What the hell/Oh shit!"

Three voices spoke at the same time—together, but separate. They were all Charlene, and at the same time, only one of them felt truly like herself. She stared up at Guy in horror, in horror, and in resigned acceptance.

"I'm a Trip/I'm a Triumvir/I'm screwed!"

CHAPTER THIRTEEN
Carol of the Bells

The ages weren't exact, but Charlene was roughly late teens, early thirties, and mid-sixties all at the same time. Her teenage self was familiar, but familiar in the same way that re-reading a book she'd read over 15 years ago was familiar—she only remembered bits as they came up. Her future self was completely foreign to her, and from what she could tell, apparently very sassy. Walzer told her that her future self wasn't exact of course—just a projection of who she might have been if she had lived, and if her life didn't take any major turns during those intervening years. Her future self was not a particularly happy person, but the template for future selves was based off of what the Ghosts of Christmas Future showed to Scrooges back on Earth, and so a little crankiness was to be expected.

Both her youngest and middle selves wore jeans, while her oldest seemed to prefer leggings, and both her youngest and oldest preferred long sleeves, her youngest in a hoodie, and her oldest in a flannel. Charlene was shocked to discover that her middle self was apparently at the peak of her fashion sense, at least based on the trajectory she'd been on when she died. She'd really thought that she'd become one of those eccentrically styl-ish older women. But apparently she was one of the ones who always looked comfortable and probably one soft chair away from a nap. She was also surprised, again, that her seemingly temporary change to her clothes continued to be permanent.

The hard part wasn't the fashion though, or getting used to seeing out of three sets of eyes. The hard part was that none of her selves were in any sort of agreement. Her youngest was profoundly unhappy, and sullen in a way only a teenager can ever properly pull off. Her oldest was the sort to want to snap at people to "just get over it" and had no patience for her youngest self. And her middle self was, well, in the middle. Also unhappy, also impatient, and just generally bewildered.

"You suck for never telling me this could happen/why didn't you tell me this could happen?/figures there was always something worse that could happen." Charlene gave Walzer three different glares. In her current state as a new Trip, he was the only one that seemed capable of following along when she talked. She was way out of alignment, he had told her, and while she hadn't thought he was all that in tune with himself, apparently, he was about as in sync as any Trip could be. Her selves tried to walk in different directions, said wildly different things even if in the same theme, and could never keep her arms from flailing all around. It was hard to control three sets of limbs. Even her eyes wouldn't behave, and she was staring at the wall, looking at Walzer, and looking just to the right of Walzer because her oldest self clearly needed glasses and refused to wear any. Making sense of the three separate perspectives was giving all three heads a headache.

"Do you have any idea how rare it is for a spirit to become a Triumvir?" Walzer asked. His youngest self seemed impressed, but the older two just alarmed. "There were three of us. Of all the spirits that have passed through here, just the three. Well, and now four."

"That you know of/three in all of time?/Rare or not, you should have said something."

Charlene's oldest self made a good point, even if it was hard for her to hear herself while she was also talking.

"In record time, no less!" Walzer continued. This time even his middle face seemed impressed, while the oldest just looked tired. "It's not that spirits haven't become Marleys, or that they haven't eventually done something to turn into Triumvirs, but to do all of that before you've even had a chance to serve as a Marley—I mean, seriously Charlene." He was amused, exasperated, and exhausted, in order of age. Charlene wondered how he got his three selves to all say the same thing, but she was still too mad to ask.

"I've been advanced since I got here/You were worried about me feeling too soon/so, I'm advanced? So what?" Charlene tried to at least get her oldest and middle selves to mimic the posture of the youngest, who refused to cooperate. After a moment, her oldest version sighed and also crossed her arms over her chest. Crossed arms were easier to manage than moving ones.

"Well, and now you have the rest of eternity to slow down!" Walzer said. "Because this is it—there's nothing after this. This is how you spend your afterlife." He huffed around his desk to his chair, his youngest form moving just slightly slower than the rest and shooting Charlene a curious look.

"Did the white liquid eat your chain too?/It's my afterlife, why do you care?" Charlene was surprised that her youngest and oldest voices synced up in their defiance. Apparently as she got older, she also regressed.

"No. You are also unique in that. I don't even know how you found that room. I didn't even know that room existed. And messing around with Christmas memories! How could you?"

One of his "how could you"s sounded more curious than mad, and Charlene's concurrent teenager nodded back in recognition. Rebel recognized rebel.

"You wouldn't understand/I wasn't interested in the memories/please, as if I'd need more memories to let go of."

"Then what?"

"I wanted to get rid of my memories, to let go of my past, and get rid of my chain." Charlene's youngest voice and oldest hadn't answered, and she felt both of them glaring, this time at herself.

"Well, you did succeed in getting rid of your chain," Walzer said, more impressed than he probably should have been. The influence of his teenager, Charlene assumed. "But this?" He waved three hands over three different bodies. "I wouldn't wish this on anyone."

It was hard to say why it was so horrible being a Trip. But Charlene understood what he meant. Never mind that the sensory input was overwhelming, the distinct selves having distinct needs and wants was enough to sink Charlene into a deep depression. How could you live in the past, the present, and the future, all at the same time? How could you ever make decisions from three different perspectives? And no one part of herself had any control over the other two, all three of them trying to take the lead. She was angry at herself on a whole new level, and frustrated, and annoyed, and disgusted and she wondered if she would ever learn to like her selves and just get along.

Plus all three had different Christmas songs in their heads. They were not mashing up well at all.

"Okay, so what now?/Now what happens?/Now what?"

"It's administration work for you," Walzer said. "Orientation and the like. There really isn't anything else to do."

Charlene mostly looked around his office, while part of her examined her nails.

"Do I have to?/Do I get an office?/Why do I have to do anything?"

"Trust me, you'll want something to do," Walzer said, and all three of his faces were in agreement about that. "And there's a training, somewhere."

He rummaged through a drawer in his desk, finally pulling out a small white sphere.

"Follow me," he said. "All of you."

Following Walzer took some doing, since two-thirds of Charlene were not feeling particularly cooperative and the middle third of her had to physically force herself to move. And then it was hard not to bump into things, and all of Walzer's office seemed surprisingly solid, or else Charlene had lost her ability to pass through objects. Ramming into the edge of his doorway hurt. He led her to the left, away from the door that she knew would lead to the Holiday Spirit Break Room, and to an office a few feet down from his on the opposite side of the hall. Charlene spotted two more doors in that direction before the hall ended in a little alcove that had two chairs and a potted plant. Two-thirds of her assumed those doors were the offices of the other two Trips, and one-third of her didn't care.

All of her looked at what was now going to be her office. She had been assured already that her little room with its little bed was gone—Trips didn't get bedrooms. Instead, they got… this.

The space was about the same as Walzer's, large enough for a couch against one wall, a large desk in the middle, and several filing cabinets on the same wall the doorway was in. Everything was grey—the door, the floor, the desk, the items on the desk, the couch, the cabinets, the ceiling—even the light looked greyish, not quite managing to be bright. Walzer walked to the desk and pushed something that opened a small hole just big enough for the sphere in his hand. He put it in, then turned to Charlene.

"You'll have to watch the whole thing," he said. "Triumvirs don't have the same freedoms as the other spirits. Good luck."

Most of his faces gave her a look of sympathy as he passed, his oldest an angry scowl. She got the impression it was going to take a while for Walzer to fully forgive her. She wished she could agree on whether or not she should worry about that.

The back wall of the office turned from grey to white, becoming a large projection screen. Black letters appeared on the wall: WELCOME TO YOUR NEW AFTERLIFE! Then the letters scrolled up, which was better than them flying at Charlene's faces. Part of her wanted to lean back against the wall, another wanted to sit on the couch, and the third wanted to head for the office chair. The wall was the closest, and since she couldn't agree on any other course, that's where she ended up, two sets of arms crossed, and one set pressed against the wall to help keep everyone balanced upright.

New words on the back wall scrolled into view: Yes, You're Dead. But what does it mean?

All of Charlene sighed. She realized that this presentation wasn't going to bring her any answers, and finally in agreement with herself, went to the couch and stretched out along its length. One part of her kept an eye on the presentation, but the other two closed their eyes.

Optimism seemed to only come in thirds. It was harder to hold on to when only one part of her felt it, so the presentation telling her that "everything is going to be okay" didn't make her feel any better. All of her was pretty sure okay was very far behind her.

Eventually she made it through the presentation, and through the rest of the orientation, and then she got to start her training to help her integrate her selves.

Charlene started with picking up a cup. Three hands reaching always almost sent the cup tumbling, or spilling whatever was inside of it, or shoving it away. So she practiced over and over again, despite her protestations that it was boring, or pointless, or stupid, or meaningless. At different times, different parts of herself had to take the lead, get herself to sit down, to focus, and to practice picking up the damn cup.

It was amazing how hard it was to get along with herself.

It was amazing how necessary it was to get along with herself in order to pick up a cup, or walk in a straight line, or have a single conversation. She never knew she had so little patience, or such a negative attitude. Or that she was so bossy. Most of her recognized that this wasn't her best self, but her self under stress, and that no one was going to be their best while dealing with everything she was dealing with. And the rest of her just felt unhappy all the time and struggled to care about anything at all.

Walzer was a great help. He talked her through the exercises he used to get himself in alignment, repeatedly focusing on small actions over and over again to get her arms and legs all working together. A series of tongue twisters helped her figure out how to speed up or slow down her speech so that all parts of her could talk together. Then he had her read to him to help her eyes focus on the same thing at the same time. The same flowy script that had befuddled her eyes when she first arrived among the Holiday Spirits didn't look obscure to her anymore, and she read it with ease, if not always in sync. There wasn't much reading selection in the Hall of Christmas Spirits, and nothing that wasn't about Christmas in some way.

Walzer favored *A Visit from St. Nicholas*, but Charlene was delighted to discover that at some point in history Christmas ghost stories—actual scary ones—were popular, and she spent a lot of time reading those.

When she wasn't reading or practicing picking up cups or

standing on one leg, Charlene was learning more about what all Walzer did. Most of his actual work duties seemed to consist of creating presentations, and he spent an inordinate amount of time fussing with font, colors, and margins. He was also preoccupied with his theory about what created the Hall of Christmas Spirits and other holiday halls, and took detailed notes from his conversations with the others, compiling notes and working out the details.

"This can't be all that you do/it's so boring," Charlene said, annoyed with herself for not agreeing on what she was going to say before she spoke. She tried again, focusing: "don't you do anything for fun?"

"Well, this is fun." Walzer clicked his pen open and closed, most of him smiling.

"What about other kinds of fun?" Charlene prodded. She recognized that part of her thought part of him was cute, but so far had been able to avoid blushing when around him. Mostly, anyway. But apparently his teenage self wasn't above flirting with her teenage self, as awkward as that was for the older parts of them, and he wagged his eyebrows at her.

"Well, there is this one thing."

Fortunately for all involved, neither young Walzer or young Charlene were particularly good at flirting, and the one thing Walzer wanted to show her was a skate park. He had a skateboard that had a snowman on back with spikes coming out of its head and its tongue sticking out aggressively. The park itself was the same grey as the office, with no real sense of it being outside or inside, but it had ramps and railings and curbs and everything a young skater could possibly need. Walzer said that Guy had made it for him, something he was very grateful for.

Charlene watched Walzer go back and forth doing tricks, and only part of her was bored. One was fascinated to watch how the three Walzer forms managed to pull off the coordination to do the tricks while giggling at the vision of his white hair blending in with the plain brown and bright green Mohawk as he sped along. The other part of her was truly, embarrassingly, impressed. She gave up trying to sync up her faces, and let them grin, cheer, and roll their eyes as they saw fit. Eventually, Charlene had the bright idea of learning to skateboard herself—not so daunting a task when you can't injure yourself—and then had to work to convince the rest of her to go along with it.

It was terrifying to try to even stand on a board, but then exhilarating to feel air whiz by her as she rolled gently down the ramp. It was the closest sensation to flying she was going to be able to have as a Trip. After that it wasn't too hard to keep talking herself into going skating. What was hard was talking herself into doing anything else.

CHAPTER FOURTEEN
The Most Wonderful Time of the Year

Time passed along, in the strange way that time passed in the Hall of Christmas Spirits, with Charlene spending her time reading, skateboarding, fiddling with presentations, and avoiding the one thing she really wanted to do.

Then there was a time when Charlene reached for her cup of coffee—an indulgence she never could quite give up and seemed to go so well in her office setting—and grabbed it without thinking, without effort, and without any sense of discord. The cup was halfway back to her desk when she realized what she had done, and how easily she had done it. There was only a moment where a part of her disagreed, but then all of her stood up.

The Hall of Christmas Spirits looked the same as when she was last in there, the tree still glittering, the candles still flickering, and the spirts all around it still chatting. Charlene wandered around the tree slowly, taking it all in and getting used to being in an old space in a new form, taking pride in the way her hands moved together and her footsteps landed squarely.

She saw Shelley's chain before she saw Shelley, and three sets of hands smoothed down three sets of clothes, a habit Charlene never had—and never would—outgrow.

"Hey, Shelley," she said, her voices strong, if various levels of nervous. Shelley turned, pulling her chains around with practiced ease. And then she smiled, and a knot that Charlene didn't even know she had inside her loosened.

"Hi honey!" she said. "You're looking swell!"

Charlene could have hugged her if her three sets of arms could agree on how to manage around Shelley's chain.

"So are you," Charlene said instead, smiling back. She spotted Jeri on the other side of Shelley and gave a wave. Her youngest self was quite pleased when Jeri waved back, and Charlene was surprised by how much more attractive she was finding the non-binary Jeri in their plain shirt and cuffed jeans. Teenage hormones were no joke. "Hi Jeri," she said, her oldest self managing to keep her youngest from sounding too excited to say hi.

"Nice nails," Jeri said, and Charlene didn't stop herself from showing off a single set of nails to the Marley.

"Thanks, I did them myself," she said, which was true, if dated information.

"Honestly, you're just adorable," Shelley said, peering at each of Charlene's faces. "I always knew you were an old soul."

"Seems like a young soul to me," Jeri said, and they winked at Charlene, sending one of her hearts a-twitter. The rest of her sighed. Did she really have to have a crush on everyone? For a moment her minds wandered in different directions as she contemplated various conclusions of said crushes, and the logistics of dating when not all of her might be into it. She spent more time than she was comfortable with thinking about how to work around chains—or incorporate them—in her dating life before pulling her thoughts back together. Two parts of her were way too old for Jeri, anyway. Shelley giggled at whatever looks this put on her faces, and Charlene shook most of her heads in response, smiling.

"It can get complicated in here," she said, motioning to her selves.

"It can get complicated out here too," Jeri said. "But complicated can be fun."

"Stop!" Shelley said, laughing as Charlene managed to blush three times over. "You're gonna scare most of her off."

Charlene wondered which ones Shelley was referring to.

"But honestly, honey. It's so good to see you."

"I was worried that maybe you wouldn't want to," Charlene said, her hands finding the edges of her sleeves and pulling on them with nervous energy. "Because…well…."

None of her knew how to finish.

"None of us want to be Marleys," Shelley said. "I don't blame you for wanting to change that. I wish I had known what you were thinking though. I could have warned you. No one thought to. Trips are just that rare."

"Seriously," Jeri added. "We were both here before Walzer, and it was shocking enough when he turned. I sort of thought he'd be the last one."

"Do you know how he did? Like what he did?"

Jeri glanced at Shelley, who shrugged back.

"No one really knows. We don't know how you did it either. Guy won't say."

Charlene contemplated this.

"I'm thinking then that maybe I shouldn't either," she said. "Though I don't agree with myself on that. If you wanted to get rid of your own chains…."

Jeri held out their hand as if to ward Charlene's words off.

"Don't tempt me," they said. "It took a long time to come to terms with being a Marley. I don't know that I have it in me to go through that kind of adjustment again. And I'm really not sure I could live with my younger self."

"It's my older self that I'd be worried about," Shelley said. "Aging was hard enough when I was alive."

Charlene nodded, but she was partly disappointed too.

"Then I won't tell," she said. "But don't ask. I am not sure I'll be able to keep it in if you do."

"Agreed," Jeri said, and Shelley nodded solemnly.

"Well, anyway," Charlene said, wincing at her transition. "What have you folks been up to?"

"Had another Earth visit. Different cousin—I have a lot of them. It went well," Jeri said.

"My niece passed," Shelley said. "We get told stuff like that. So that's really it for me and my trips to Earth."

"I'm so sorry, Shell," Charlene said. "What happens now?"

The other specter shrugged.

"Same thing as always I guess. There's chatting, and chain rattling, and egg-nog. If only it was spiked!"

"If only!" Charlene agreed.

"I'd drink to that," Jeri said, and again Shelley wondered if they were even old enough to. Though she also supposed drinking ages didn't really count after dying.

"But I'll be okay, honey," Shelley said. "I've been preparing for this. Got a nice stash of memories coming to me. They'll help pass the time. And I got you now, and Jeri, and some others." She smiled. "As long as you got friends, what else do you need?"

Charlene and Jeri smiled back at her, but most of Charlene felt very sad. She could tell Shelley about the white liquid, she told herself. Being a Trip wasn't so bad.

But even she couldn't convince herself of that lie. Chains were heavy, but feeling split all the time was worse.

"Speaking of friends," Shelley said, looking at someone behind Charlene. Two of Charlene's heads tried to turn in two opposite directions to look, and for a moment she got very dizzy, reaching out hands randomly to catch her balance.

Guy grasped one of her hands, and helped her steady.

"Focus on just my arm," he said as Charlene wrestled with herself, finally getting all her bits headed in the same directions, three hands holding Guy's arm.

"I'm so sorry," she said, all her voices filled with genuine remorse and embarrassment. "I haven't had a split like that in a while. I wouldn't have come out if…"

"Oh honey, is that why it took so long?" Shelley asked. "You didn't have to. We would have understood."

"No reason to hide who you are," Jeri added. "Or what."

But Charlene was afraid to look at Guy. The last time she'd seen him, he had looked so sad.

"We'll take you any way you are," he said, and all six of her eyes found a way to meet both of his. He was smiling. Charlene hadn't realized until then just how much she missed seeing his smile.

"I wish I had been as accepting of myself," she said, and two parts of her self immediately wished she could take it back. Her oldest sent them chiding energy. "I wish I had done a lot of things differently," she said.

Then she realized that she was still holding Guy's arm, and new feelings flooded through her as she let go, hands smoothing clothes and eyes struggling to look up.

"What's done is done," Guy said. "And now you have a new job to do."

"Oh yeah?"

"There's a new Christmas Spirit coming in—and he's assigned to you."

Charlene felt most of herself freeze while her oldest self nodded.

"I'm ready," she said firmly, aware that she was trying to convince herself.

"You wouldn't have gotten an assignment if you weren't," Guy said. He held out his arm expectantly.

Charlene wished that were true, but parts of her doubted it. She nodded anyway, shooting Shelley and Jeri goodbye looks as she took Guy's arm again, but for a very different purpose.

Then they were in her office instantaneously, and Walzer greeted them, all three of his faces beaming with excitement as he held a grey folder out to Charlene.

"Another Christmas one," he said. "Horrible situation with hanging up lights. Mid-forties, father of three. How are you going to do it?"

Charlene didn't have time to be sad about the man's details, taking the folder and flipping through it, spotting a picture of a smiling man with straight black hair cut neatly above his ears, light brown eyes, and smooth tan skin. Gani Hill, she read. He had a nice smile.

"I want to start with a visit," she said. She had contemplated this long and hard, and she really did feel, in retrospect, that seeing the younger version of herself did help her when she was trying to adjust to being dead. "And no scrolling presentation."

"No presentation?" Two-thirds of Walzer was shocked.

"Cue cards," Charlene said, "paper sized. And a white board where I can write down the answers to his questions, in case he can't hear yet." She looked at Guy, as if asking for approval, and he smiled back at her.

"Sounds good. Are you ready?"

Charlene went to her desk and pulled out the cards she'd prepared, along with a small white board and a set of markers that she shoved into her jacket pocket. She wished she had a satchel of some kind for all her supplies.

"Wait," she said. "I need one more thing." Then she closed her eyes and concentrated. How many times had she watched Guy pull his hat or jacket out of thin air? And she'd changed her clothes, and floated through doors. Charlene was pretty sure this was in her ghost skill set, even if she hadn't done anything exactly like this before. A bag was just an addition to an outfit. It shouldn't be that hard. She opened her eyes when she felt pressure on her right shoulder and left hip.

It was a nice brown leather satchel with a large front flap, and she was able to easily put all her supplies in it, taking markers from her pocket and putting them into a side pouch instead.

"Okay, I'm ready," she said, looking up. But Walzer was looking at her strangely, and Guy's face was unreadable. "What? Did I do something wrong?"

Charlene twisted to look around her, and checked in with all her selves, seeing if arms and legs were lined up. They were. "Unique New York," she said, testing her voice, but all was right there too. She looked back at Guy and Walzer.

"You made a bag," Walzer said.

"I changed my clothes too," she said. "I mean, when I was a Marley, but still. Same principle."

"Not, actually, the same thing at all," Guy said. Was he worried? Surprised? She wished he would smile or joke or something. Three sets of eyes, and none of them were able to interpret what they were seeing in Guy's face.

"Don't we need to hurry? I mean, I know time moves differently here, but…"

"Yes," Guy said, moving and seeming to break whatever spell he was in. He put out his arm again. Charlene walked over to him, still trying to get a read on Walzer.

"Are you going to wish me luck?" she asked.

"Good luck," he said. But his faces couldn't make up their minds about his feelings, and she thought at least one of them looked awed. "You will do remarkably," he said.

Charlene thought it was an odd choice of words. But she put her hands on Guy's arms and was whisked away, and then she didn't have time to worry about Walzer.

CHAPTER FIFTEEN
What Christmas Means to Me

Charlene was surrounded by white light. It was a familiar type of glow, and she watched as the light seemed to dim to reveal Gani Hill standing in front of her and Guy. He was not much taller than Charlene, and had a roundness to his features and body that suggested comfortable living. In that moment, he was still, but when Charlene was ready for him to he would be able to move, to sense, and be aware. She had been told all about this in the presentation Walzer made her watch about being a Trip. The presentation didn't have all the answers though, and Charlene pulled nervously at the strap of her bag.

"How do we do this?" Charlene asked. Guy took a small object out of his pocket and handed it to Charlene. She recognized it as one of the ornaments filled with memory.

"That's your template," he said. Startled, Charlene almost dropped the ornament, but one set of hands was able to hold on.

"Me? Walzer said that you created the memory when I first died."

"Walzer can't do what you can," Guy said. "Look at it, and then create it."

"I don't have a Memory Machine," Charlene said, looking around to confirm her statement.

"You didn't have a bag either, but then you did. You can do this." Guy pushed his hat up a little so that Charlene could see the encouragement in his eyes.

She turned the ornament over in her hands. This one happened to be blue, and like the last time she touched one, the material inside was moving quickly in response to her touch. She lifted it to her eyes and was grateful for all the time Walzer made her read, as she was able to focus her gazes to see something unfolding inside the swirling substance. The way the liquid moved suggested shapes, and she peered in closer to try to see them, mesmerized by the ebb and flow, wondering if whatever was inside the glass was actually pulsing or if she just imagined it was. As she stared longer and longer, becoming more and more entranced by the shapes, they grew bigger—or she grew smaller—until she was at a scale to see the images clearly. The blue dissolved into faint colors, like someone had painted over black and white film, and she could finally see clearly a younger version of Gani rushing with hands full of plates to a small table, where a much older man sat alone slumped over a newspaper.

"Here you are Mr. Clarkson," Gani said, arranging the plates around the table to maximize the space. The fact that Gani knew the customer's name suggested that he was either a regular or someone very important. "Let me know if you need anything else."

"I'm going to need you to work Christmas," Mr. Clarkson said, absently picking up his fork and poking at one of the dishes in front of him. "Lorene has that thing with her mother, and

Sandra is working Christmas Eve and New Year's Eve."

If Gani was upset by this news, he didn't show it.

"No problem, Mr. Clarkson," he said. He rushed off and returned shortly with a pitcher of water, refilling Mr. Clarkson's glass.

"Thank you, Gani," Mr. Clarkson said. "Of course you'll get holiday pay." He looked up at his server. "And I really do appreciate your willingness to help out."

"Any time, Mr. Clarkson," Gani said. "You know how much I love this place."

Charlene pulled back from the image, and it felt like it took a long time until she could see the blue in the ornament again.

"Why this memory?" she asked Guy.

"I'm not sure which memory it is," Guy confessed. "But it's linked with this one." He handed her another ornament, the substance inside red and cheery.

"How does the Memory Machine work?" she asked. Trips weren't allowed to use it. Something about their triplication rendered the mechanism useless.

"You don't need it," Guy said.

"Yes, but how does it work?" she asked again, peering into the red and seeing shapes move around.

"The way the person using it expects it to."

Charlene considered this. She had been thinking about this a lot, actually, especially during all the times that Walzer talked about his pet theory—how the afterlife was built on belief.

She needed a bag, and then she made one. She needed to figure out how to make this memory come to life too.

Charlene stood back then and threw the blue-filled ornament as hard as she could directly in front of Gani. The glass shattered into confetti and the blue spilled out, pouring in all directions and filling up the space in front of him, getting bigger and bigger, the substance stretching thinner and thinner, getting paler as it went until it was as light as a midday sky. Then it lightened still, dark shapes in it revealing themselves as Young-Gani holding plates, and Mr. Clarkson at his table.

Charlene was shocked at herself, but mostly proud. She looked at Guy, who had a peculiar look on his face, and felt a sting of disappointment. She thought he would be excited about what she achieved. He nodded at her to indicate she should keep going, so she turned back to Gani. After another moment of indecision, Charlene picked an action and committed to it.

"Wake," Charlene breathed, putting all her intention behind the word.

Now-Gani blinked his eyes. Then he moved his hand, and it was clear he could not yet see it.

"See," whispered Charlene, and she watched Now-Gani blink his eyes some more, stare at his hand, touch his face, open his mouth to scream. She waited until he seemed screamed out, and then spoke again: "hear and remember."

The shapes in front of Now-Gani started to move, and Charlene watched Now-Gani watch his younger self in shock and awe. She watched him reach out a tentative hand only to see his younger self pass right through it.

Charlene looked around to see Guy's reaction to this but

couldn't see the trainer anywhere. Part of her was alarmed by that, but most was focused on her work, so she stepped closer to Gani.

"Do you remember this?" she asked, catching Now-Gani's attention.

"Holy smokes, what is happening?" he asked. She smiled warmly at him, and was pleased that all of her was working together on this.

"It's okay. I want you to concentrate, if you can. And look," she pointed at the image of Then-Gani refilling Mr. Clarkson's water glass. "Do you remember this?"

Now-Gani nodded.

"Good," Charlene said. "Was he a kind man, Mr. Clarkson?"

"One of the best bosses I ever had," Now-Gani said. He watched his younger self laughing with Mr. Clarkson, a big hearty laugh that the older man shared. "I loved that man."

"Interesting," Charlene said. She looked down at the second ornament in her hand. "Want to see what happens next?"

"Oh yes please!" Now-Gani said, excitedly. "If you show me what I hope you will show me."

"Let's find out!" Charlene said, and she threw the red-filled ornament down in the same place as the last one, and watched with growing fascination as the red liquid spread out and up, covering the images beneath it and slowly fading from red to pink to clear as new images emerged.

Then-Gani was in the restaurant again, only this time he wasn't rushing. There weren't that many customers and almost all the ones in attendance were sitting alone. She watched Then-Gani put a dish down at an empty table and take a moment to clear his hair from his eyes and straighten the apron wrapped around his waist before picking up the plate and plastering on a particularly wide smile.

"Here you go, miss," he said. "I hope you won't be sorry that you picked the special."

The young woman sitting at the table matched his smile with a wide one of her own, putting down a book she had been reading to do so.

"Oh, I have a good feeling about this," she said. "You wouldn't have recommended it if you didn't think it was good."

"That's Vera, my wife," Now-Gani said. "I mean, she wasn't back then. That was our first time meeting. Now, she's my wife."

Charlene studied his face, trying to get a sense of what he was feeling. He was smiling—not as wide or as care-free as his younger self and the younger version of his wife. But still, smiling. He was leaning forward, watching with great interest, moving his lips along to the words his younger self was saying as if he'd relived this moment already a million times. The look on his face could only be described by one word: joy.

Eventually the scene before them played out, resetting itself to the first moment, Then-Gani frozen with a plate in his hand.

"Can I see it again?" Now-Gani asked, turning to Charlene and seeing her for the first time. If he was alarmed by her triplicate state, he gave no indication.

"Uh, sure," Charlene said. "But there's some things you should know."

"I'm dead, aren't I?" he said quietly. "I didn't think I'd survive that fall. And then when I saw this—" he motioned to the memory in front of him. "Is this heaven?"

"No," Charlene said, taken aback. "Were you very religious?"

"No," he admitted, ducking his head down as if trying to dodge blushing. "But getting to relive that, I just thought…."

"It's all a bit more complex than that," Charlene said. "The short of it is that you're dead, and there's an afterlife, and believe it or not, such as thing as Christmas Spirits. And now you're one of them."

"A Christmas Spirit? Really?" Now-Gani looked over at this past self. "Well that fits. I met the love of my life on Christmas. Now I get to celebrate Christmas for all eternity." He grinned. "So, can I watch it again?"

Charlene wasn't sure that this was how this was supposed to go. She also wasn't sure if she could replay the memory again, but when she looked around and still didn't see Guy, she figured she ought to at least give it a try.

"Sure thing," she said. Then, not knowing what else to do, she focused on the memory and said, very forcefully: "again."

The figures started to move again, and Now-Gani clapped his hands together in delight, like a little kid.

After the fifth time watching it, she persuaded him that enough was enough and that it was time to move on.

"Great, where to next?" he asked. Not sure what else to

do, Charlene held out her arm, and motioned for him to take it, which he did, like she was about to lead him to a formal dance.

"Now," she said, only part of her hesitating, "The Hall of Christmas Spirits."

CHAPTER SIXTEEN
Joy to the World

It had been surprisingly easy to talk Gani through his orientation, and his trip through his own history to the main Hall of the Spirits was lovely and joyful, as he showed off his childhood home and the first place he lived with his wife after they were married. Jeri joined them to give him his warning about becoming a Marley and he caught on quickly, and spent some time asking polite questions about their chains and experience as a ghost before looking back up at Charlene expectantly. So she took him to the Ghosts of Christmas Past, nervously presenting him to Nomura and the others.

Fortunately, it wasn't Nomura's turn to go down to Earth, so one of the others took Gani with him.

"We would have expected Guy, not you," Nomura said.

"I know," Charlene said. "I haven't seen him since he took me to meet Gani." She pulled at her sleeves anxiously. "This is my first assignment. Somehow I thought he'd be more…involved."

"Walzer would not have been doing these things," Nomura said, clearly as curious as Charlene was.

"I know," Charlene said again. "But I don't know what is happening any more than you do. I'm just trying to do right by Gani. I hope he does okay."

"He would not have been like you," Nomura said, a flash of her old anger coming out. "He would have listened."

"He's happier," Charlene said. "Just wants to help."

Nomura stared at Charlene's faces for a long moment, and Charlene was worried about what she was looking for, or what she was seeing.

"You would not have been happy," Nomura said. With her vocal tic, Charlene was unsure what tense Nomura actually meant, but Charlene nodded anyway. She hadn't been happy on Earth, and she wouldn't have been happy as a Ghost of Christmas Past. She would never have gotten over the temptation to see her loved ones.

"We would have had Gani stay a while," she said. "We would have liked him to shadow many of us."

"Sure," Charlene said. "I'll check back with you in a bit."

Nomura nodded, satisfied.

"And Nomura—I really am sorry that I left you."

Nomura shrugged.

"It would have not been what it would not have been."

Charlene took a second to translate that as "it is what it is" and grinned. Nomura was right—it was what it was. And it was in the past, now.

Charlene apparated back to her office and dumped her bag full of supplies on her couch, having mixed feelings about not needing them. Then she walked over to Walzer's office, because she didn't think he'd be okay with her literally popping up into his space. He looked up when she entered, two of his faces frowning, the third's eyes bright with curiosity.

"You're alone," he said.

"Yeah, I don't know what happened to Guy," Charlene said. "But Gani—my trainee—did great! He ended up with a happy Christmas memory, and it really seemed to make him feel better about dying."

"Oh," Walzer said. "I wouldn't have thought of that."

"I wouldn't have either, but it worked great," Charlene said, flopping all of her selves onto his couch. "I really think we need to rethink this whole orientation process. We've been trying to focus on getting them okay with being Christmas Spirits first, when really we should be concentrating on getting them okay with dying first, and then teach them all about this Christmas Spirit thing."

"I suppose," Walzer said. He leaned back against his desk, his arms crossed and his faces thoughtful. "You didn't pick the memory? I picked yours."

"No, Guy just had them ready…."

"Them?"

"There were two of them, linked. The first started off with this old dude, Mr. Clarkson, telling Gani he'd have to work Christmas. Classic Scrooge behavior. But instead, he was actually super nice and paid double time, and then on Christmas day…" Two parts of Charlene had stopped talking before the third one caught up. Walzer did not look okay.

"None of this sounds right. None of this sounds anything like how it's done. I picked your memory, and Guy made it for me. And it was one, only one. I wasn't allowed to pick two."

Charlene struggled to get all three selves sitting up at the same time, but finally they were back in alignment.

"Did I screw up again?" she asked. "Is that why Guy disappeared?"

Walzer shook all of his heads.

"You'd better go find Guy," he said. "All of this is above my paygrade."

"Wait," Charlene said as most of her stood up. "We get paid?"

"Figure of speech," Walzer said. "Go, find Guy."

Charlene nodded and rushed out, waiting until she was in the hallway before closing her eyes and picturing her destination.

She appeared in the corner of the Holiday Spirit Break Room, not far from where she first saw Guy. She looked around, even did a quick circuit of the room, but didn't see him. With three sets of eyes, there was no way she could miss him. So she closed all six eyes and focused again.

This time when she opened her eyes she was in the Hall of Christmas Spirits, staring at the tree. Part of her really wanted to go look at the ornaments, and yet another part of her kind of wanted to throw more of them around, but she reeled those parts in and walked around the tree, passing Shelley and Jeri.

"How'd it go, honey?" Shelley asked. Charlene gave her six thumbs up.

"Ridiculously well," she said. "But have you seen Guy?"

Shelley and Jeri both said no, and while it was clear they had more questions, Charlene kept walking, all of her eyes searching everywhere. But there was no fedora, no suit, no sign of Guy.

Charlene turned away from the tree and toward the white pearlescent door. She had thought of that place as off limits ever since the white liquid moment, but she also didn't know where else to look. Eyes closed, a moment of concentration, and then eyes open again to stare at the white and gold arms of the Memory Machine. It was dutifully plucking memories and encasing them in glass. Guy was not with it.

Charlene looked up. She couldn't imagine that Guy could ever want to be in the strange room with the white pool, but part of her admitted that wasn't the only reason why she wanted to go back there.

It barely took a blink to transport herself.

The pool was just where she remembered it being, white and gold arms plucking white blobs from it, a black conveyor belt moving those blobs away.

Guy was standing in front of the pool, staring at it.

"You okay?" Charlene asked. There was something about the tension in his back that she didn't trust.

"I'd never seen it do that," he said. He turned enough to look over his shoulder and catch Charlene's eyes—a moment of acknowledgement, she realized—and then went back to staring at the pool and to what he was saying. "Dissolve a chain like that. In fact, I'd never seen anything like this." He gestured to the arms and the conveyor belt.

"I don't understand," Charlene said, cautiously walking up beside him. "Doesn't it always look like this?"

"The pool is always here," he said. "And there is always

some way for the memories to leave the pool and become ornaments. The ornaments themselves are consistent, because of the tree. But these mechanical arms…" He poked one with a finger. "You have a hell of an imagination," he said.

Charlene stared up at him.

"I don't understand."

"Don't you?"

Charlene's eyes searched the corners of the room, the pool, the mechanical arms for some scrap of understanding. There had been something about her afterlife, from the first moment that she saw her younger self in her first job out of college, that felt different. And it wasn't being a Christmas Spirit, or meeting Walzer and Guy and Shelley and the others. *She* was different. She'd been exceptional from the moment that she died.

"What would happen if I stepped into the pool?" she asked. She wasn't sure why she was asking, and parts of her were scared. But she also wasn't scared.

"I honestly don't know."

"It really is all about belief, isn't it?" she asked. Things were starting to click, but they were clicking across three separate minds and she hadn't put them all together yet. "This room looks the way I believed it would look. It was called a Memory Machine so I imagined a machine." She touched one of the arms with two of her right hands, the third drifting up to brush hair out of her eyes. "And I wanted a way to get rid of my chains. And a way to show Gani his memories—without a machine. And a bag. I wanted a bag."

"And you made a bag."

"And I made a bag," she repeated. She stood very close to Guy, her shoulders almost touching his arm. "Who are you?"

"A trainer," he said. "Like I've always said."

He moved toward her, closing the gap, and she felt the heat of his body three times over.

"And how did you become a trainer?" One of her hands twisted, searched, found his. The other two followed suit.

"I wanted a hat," he said. "It completed the outfit. But I hadn't died with a hat. Or my jacket."

"Was there another trainer, before you?"

"He moved on."

"Where did he go?" She was practically whispering now, her low tones matching his, his fingers wrapped around hers.

"Wherever we go next." He squeezed her hand, whether out of comfort or fear, she couldn't tell.

"Are you going to leave?"

He turned to face her then, pushing his hat back on his head with his free hand, and wrapping the other one around her backs, pulling her closer toward him.

"How could I?" he asked. "Not when I've finally found you, someone else like me. Someone who I could really share all of this with. I have been so alone, for so long. But from the moment I met you, there was something. And I hoped. I also feared, because your path didn't look like mine. I never was a Marley, or a Trip."

"Then I *am* like you," Charlene said, the past bits starting to come together. "Another trainer." It was amazing to think that, to hear Guy talk to her like this, to have him so close to her.

Charlene didn't want to be three people anymore. She wished with all her heart that there was just one of her, because she couldn't figure out how to kiss Guy with three sets of lips.

So she closed her eyes, and focused. She felt the light touch of Guy's hand on her cheek and realized with a start that she had only one cheek. She opened a single pair of eyes to stare up into his deep brown ones. She was completely and fully integrated, three turned back into one.

"You did it," he said. "I knew you would." He pulled her closer, his face mere centimeters away from hers.

"I'm too jealous to let you kiss three of me," she said, smiling. He laughed, and she pushed up on her toes so that she could press her lips against his. His mouth was warm and tender, and his lips pressed back, gentle and firm at the same time. Then he deepened the kiss, his tongue exploring in ways that set all her nerves on fire. It was a long moment before they separated again, and then Charlene struggled to let him go.

But there was one more thing she needed to do.

"I have to find out," she said. "Because I think it's important. Because I think I almost have it, and there is only one piece missing."

He nodded, but his eyes were sad. She realized then that for all his warmth, he had always had a touch of sadness about him, a touch of loneliness.

"Am I really the first one like you?" she asked.

"Since my trainer left, yes."

"And there can be two of us, right? There doesn't just have to be one?"

"Not anymore," he said. "You keep breaking all the rules." He grinned. "I am so glad that you keep breaking all the rules."

"Me too."

"You'll come back," he said. It wasn't a question. He took his hat off and put in on her head. "You have to come back now."

Charlene adjusted the hat, and grinned at him.

"Now I know I can do anything."

"The hat isn't magic."

"Says you." She stood up on her toes again for another, shorter kiss, and then pulled away from him, struggling to let go of his hand. He seemed just as reluctant as she was.

"Do you really have to?"

Charlene looked over at the pool. There were answers there to questions she couldn't even articulate but felt through every fiber of her being. She really did have to.

"I never could let anything go," she said, and Guy laughed.

"Me included?"

"Definitely."

Then Charlene stepped forward. All three selves integrated or not, she was still of at least two minds about this. But she kept walking anyway.

The first step into the white liquid didn't burn the way she feared it might, but sent radiating waves of warmth up her legs. Walking forward was easier after that, and soon she was up to her knees, then her waist. And then she dived in the rest of the way, completely submerging herself.

Charlene was surrounded by warmth. She swam easily through it, her eyes open to the brightness of it, her mouth and nose breathing it in, and with it, memories:

Then-Charlene snuck around the corner and into the living room of her childhood home, seeing a short squat tree covered in homemade decorations, piles of presents all around it, her older sister's hand warm in hers.

Then-Charlene watched as her best friend Jonelle picked up the bottle of wine they had been drinking all night, and held it like a microphone between the two of them as they sang together, "and though it's been said, many times, many way…"

Then-Charlene felt arms wrap around her from behind as she looked up into her boyfriend Stephen's face, and he nodded to the mistletoe above them, then spun her around in his arms for a kiss.

Then-Charlene popped a piece of homemade fudge into her mouth as she watched her father and mother laugh while struggling to wrap a large box with a pink and purple dollhouse pictured on the side of it in red and green paper.

Then-Charlene walked back from her favorite lunch spot on a cold December day in New York City, carrying a gaudy fake table-top tree back to her office.

And Charlene realized that it didn't matter what happened before or next, because each memory that washed over her had one thing in common: joy. Lights, and trees, and presents, and family, and friends, and food, and cold, and warmth, and joy, and joy, and joy, and joy.

Life had ended, but the chances for joy hadn't.

Charlene swam for the surface of the pool, finally ready to make new memories.

The End

Dear Reader,

Word-of-mouth is crucial for any author to succeed. If you enjoyed the book, please leave a review on Amazon. Even if it's just a sentence or two. It would make all the difference and would be very much appreciated:
www.amazon.com, search for: J.M. Phillippe
Thank you!

J.M. Phillippe

Want more holiday adventures?

Try a sneak peek of...

BLUE
CHRISTMAS
A HOLIDAY ROMANCE

BETHANY MAINES

BLUE CHRIJTMAJ

Jake Garner's Apartment

Blue Jones set down her plastic bins and approached the lock box. Time to find out if Mr. J. Garner and significant other ever changed their key code. She typed in 3-9-4-8 and the little door of the box popped open with a soft click. She reached in with gentle fingers and pulled out the condo key as if scared she might frighten it back into hiding.

Blue put the key in the front door lock and tried to avoid eye contact with the cheerful reindeer hanging just at head height. It looked old, like someone's beloved and traditional decoration. She took a deep breath, fighting against the kick of adrenaline and guilt. Walking through someone else's home always gave her a sick little thrill. It was the worst kind of invasion of privacy—prying into all their drawers and poking in the odd corners of someone's life, unwelcomed and uninvited—but instead of feeling fear and shame she felt excited and dangerous. The only thing she really felt ashamed about was what came next—stealing.

Blue turned the key and let the door swing open.

She was immediately hit by a wave of foul air and a pan-icked barking from inside the condo. Blue covered her mouth and nose with her hand. Mr. J. Garner was an occasional user of the pet walking and sitting services of Blue's employer: Rover Sit Stay. She had cribbed his key box code out of his file and double checked on Facebook that he and his partner were out of the country for a three-day weekend. She'd also double checked whether or not they'd booked pet sitting services.

They had not.

At the time Blue had assumed that they had chosen to take their dog with them.

Blue grabbed her tote bins and dropped them in the condo entryway. She slammed the door shut and went deeper into the condo, looking for the origination of the stink.

In the living room, the plastic khaki dog crate was shaking as she approached. Blue bent down and looked inside. A black and white French Bulldog with a white spot over one eye whimpered and huddled in the back of the crate. He was covered in poop and his water and food bowls were empty.

"Those bastards," swore Blue.

She looked around the room. The condo was manly. It had man couches in leather and a blocky man coffee table in wood. Even the Christmas tree in the corner was a hefty cone shape instead of the spindly Noble Fir that designers preferred. But over the top of the condo someone had dabbed pink bits of femininity like cupcake sprinkles. The couch had fluffy white and ornate brocade pillows, neither of which looked comfortable.

For a moment she contemplated simply letting the dog out to rub his poor stinking body all over the furniture, but she quickly realized that this would result in her touching dog poop at some point. She also couldn't leave the dog in that state.

She grabbed the large crate pushed it across the living room and wedged it into the bathroom doorway. Then she reached over the top and opened the metal grate door. The dog sprinted out into the bathroom, his nails scrabbling on the tile. Blue hopped over the crate and grabbed the dog gingerly by his pink rhinestone encrusted collar. She dragged him into the glass walled shower, turning on the water before shutting the door with a quick slam. A few minutes later she opened the door a crack and looked in. The Frenchie looked miserable in the corner of the shower. Fortunately, the shower had a hose attachment and she was able to rinse him off from the doorway. When he was somewhat clean, she stripped down to her underwear and went in and then used the most expensive looking bottle of shampoo in the shower and scrubbed him down. When the dog was finally clean, Blue turned him loose into the bathroom, then dragged the crate into the shower to rinse it off too.

As much as she disliked the idea of cleaning up dog crap for these horrible people who couldn't be bothered to book a dog sitter for a three-day weekend, she refused to let the dog suffer because they were evil. Besides, at this point, she was going to steal everything that wasn't nailed down. Dog abuse ranked high on her list of things that should be paid for with prompt and horrible retribution.

Blue put her clothes back on and gave the dog some water, before taking a quick tour of the apartment while the Frenchie attempted to inhale his entire water bowl.

Ordinarily, this was the part she hated. She liked the voyeuristic experience of being in the fancy houses she visited, but the part where she decided which items she was going to steal made her feel dirty. Someone had worked hard for these things and she was about to walk off with them. She looked in the second bedroom again. All the dog toys were located in this room along with every electronic gadget she could think of and several she couldn't identify. The equipment was professional grade. There were video cameras, mics, everything someone could need to make a movie. It would probably bring a mint, but that looked like someone's livelihood. She had previously vowed never to screw up someone's living. She only wanted items that were extra—things that were unnecessary to life. The seven-hundred-dollar towel warmer from last month sprang to mind. But again, that was what she *usually* did. Such kindness was for people who bothered to book a dog sitter instead of leaving a dog locked in a crate for three days with no food or water.

She had just decided to start loading electronics into her bins when the dog came out of the bathroom and went to the front door, staring at it intently.

"Buddy, I don't have time to take you for a walk. I've already been here a lot longer than I meant to."

The dog didn't budge. Blue growled in unhappiness. Finally, she stomped into the kitchen and grabbed the leash off the hook.

"OK," she said to the dog. "But we have to be quick."

The dog panted up at her. Now that he was no longer covered in his own feces, Blue could see that he had JACQUES embroidered on his magenta gem studded collar.

"Seriously, Jacques," she said shutting the door behind her and pocketing the key, "I know you've been locked up for a day and a half, but you've got to pee quickly."

Jacques took off for the stairwell, clearly in agreement. Blue hurried down the stairs trying to keep up with Jacques and exited at a dash, almost crashing into an Amazon.com looking bro in a suit.

"Hey," he said pointing at the dog, "that's Jake's dog."

"He's out of town," said Blue. "I'm taking Jacques for a walk."

"Cool," said the man, running his eyes over her figure, in a way that made her feel slimed. "I'm in 403 if you need anything."

"Thanks," she said, with a tight smile. "Gotta go." She gave Jacques a little more leash and let him run. The bro waved as she jogged off. "Well," she said quietly to Jacques, "since I don't need a douchebag, I guess I won't be going there."

Jacques ignored her, homing in on a pee-able tree. Blue jogged with Jacques until he slowed to a leisurely stroll and turned every tree and bush into a sniff stop, then she turned around and brought him reluctantly back to the condo. Once inside she returned the leash to the hook in the kitchen.

The kitchen was a stainless-steel concrete counter top

kind of place. And Blue thought it had an empty feeling as if it wasn't really used. Curious, she opened the fridge. It was full of veggies and staples and then an entire shelf of diet shakes. Blue made a disgusted face and slammed the door shut. On the front of the fridge was a "happy couple" picture, half-covered by a pizza coupon. The guy, listed as J. Garner in the dog sitting database, looked as though he'd been purchased from the ruggedly good-looking department. Which was annoying because dog abusers should be hideous and deformed so that they could be spotted while walking down the street. She looked at the woman and decided she knew who the diet shakes belonged to. The blonde, pouty lipped, bronzed woman on the fridge looked like she probably insta-filtered every selfie on social media.

Blue tried not to hate, but the diet shake drinker was probably a size one who needed to diet like she needed another botox injection. If the blonde's lips got any bigger, they could probably be used as a flotation device. Blue tried to remind herself that this was fine. Everyone had a right to self-improvement. Blue always wanted to improve her little tummy roll. It was just that some part of her got bitter and jealous of the people who could afford to buy instant improvements.

"Your mommy is a Basic bitch, isn't she?" said Blue, looking down at Jacques. He dropped a ball on her foot. She booted it out into the hall. She heard it pong off the walls and watched as Jacques dashed after it, his nails digging into the wood floor. With a smile, she turned and pushed through a swinging door into the living room. She began to separate out the plastic tubs she'd brought. In her experience, no one questioned the removal of items in plastic bins. Toting out items by hand raised eyebrows. Well-packed items in tubs looked like a donation to a local charity. She even had business cards with a fake charity on them – The Giving Society. The phone number went to a pizza place in Kent, but it would look real for the thirty seconds she needed it to.

The first time Blue had stolen something she'd been in a full panic. She'd just received a final notice on her grandmother's house, the utility bill, and an invoice from the hospital for twelve thousand dollars. She'd arrived in tears at her pet sitting gig and found a lovely note from the home owner.

HELP YOURSELF TO THE OPEN BOTTLE OF WINE. IT NEEDS TO BE DRUNK BEFORE WE'LL BE BACK!

She'd downed half a bottle of wine and then lost Mr. Mittens under the couch. When she'd bent over to retrieve the recalcitrant cat out from under the furniture, she'd seen it: the very dusty, older model iPad. She'd picked it up with shaking fingers, and reset it to factory mode. Three hours and a trip to a pawn shop later Blue sent in a payment to the utility company. Over the next two days she'd made a list of all the places she'd ever pet sit for. She'd selected the clients that she hadn't worked for in over a year, stalked them on social media, found the ones who were away for the summer holidays and then walked through and taken the items that coalesced at the center of the Venn diagram of expensive, least likely to be missed, and easiest to pawn. By the end of the week she'd made the mortgage payment and was in negotiations with the hospital for a payment plan.

She'd repeated the operation at the next major holiday season. Carefully scamming info from the dog sitting database at Rover Sit Stay and fellow dog walkers so that it wasn't only her clients that were getting hit. Blue had found over the last year and a half that with careful planning and care she could actually get away with taking several thousand dollars-worth of goods from a house and the home owner might not even notice she'd been there.

She didn't feel good about it, but on the other hand she and her grandmother weren't out on the street and they hadn't had to stop Grandma's cancer treatments. If she could just finish out her master's degree and get a real, decent paying job, then maybe she could stop doing this.

Jacques reappeared, prancing on his toes, proud of his ball recovery skills. With a laugh she took the ball and tossed it again. He gleefully chased it into a bag full of Christmas presents by the door into the kitchen.

"No, Jacques!" she exclaimed as he scratched at the pretty paper. She did have some standards—she didn't steal Christmas presents, even from dog abusers. "No!" He evaded her reaching hands and dove back to the bag. "Just let me get it!" She reached into the bag, trying to block his furry body from going into the tote. He barely complied, hovering near her head and panting loudly in her ear. "Goofy pooch," she said, retrieving the ball from the bag and standing up. Only then did she hear the sound of footsteps in the kitchen. She turned, toward the sound, horrified as the door opened and a dark figure came hurtling through.

She shrieked as they went down in a tangle of limbs. Then there was silence and she lay on the living room floor panting with a very large, heavy man resting on top of her, face down on her chest.

Blue Christmas is available from any online book retailer. Or learn more at: www.BethanyMaines.com

Blue Zephyr Press

Enjoy other books from Blue Zephyr Press!

THE FAARIAN CHRONICLES: EXILE

by Karen Harris Tully

Fifteen-year-old Sunny Price dreams of being an Olympic gymnast, but thanks to the worst custody agreement in the universe, she finds out she's half-alien and is exiled to her absentee-mother's home planet. She has to give up her friends and elite gymnastics career to live with a mother who only wants to give orders? This. Sucks.

AN UNSEEN CURRENT

by Bethany Maines

You never know what's beneath the surface. When Seattle native and ex-actress Tish Yearly finds herself fired and evicted all in one afternoon, she knows she's in deep water. And when she discovers the strangled corpse of grandfather's best friend, she knows she's in over her head. Now Tish must swim against the current, and depend on her nearly forgotten acting skills to stay alive.

blue zephyrpress.com

J.M. Phillippe is the author of the novels *Perfect Likeness* and *Aurora One* and the short stories: *The Sight* and *Plane Signals*. She has lived in the deserts of California, the suburbs of Seattle, and the mad rush of New York City. She works as a clinical social worker in Brooklyn, New York and spends her free time binge-watching quality TV, drinking cider with amazing friends, and learning the art of radical self-acceptance, one day at a time.

Find out more at:

JennaePhillippe.com